KW-795-918

AIM BEFORE YOU DRAW

T. M. DOLAN

A Black Horse Western

ROBERT HALE • LONDON

© *T.M. Dolan 1996*
First published in Great Britain 1996

ISBN 0 7090 5891 8

Robert Hale Limited
Clerkenwell House
Clerkenwell Green
London EC1R 0HT

The right of T.M. Dolan to be identified as author of this
work has been asserted by her in accordance with
the Copyright, Designs and Patents Act 1988.

HAMPSHIRE COUNTY LIBRARY

F   0 7090 5891 8

C012960324

FLEET LIBRARY
TEL: 614213

Typeset in Times by Pitfold Design, Hindhead, Surrey.
Printed in Great Britain by St Edmundsbury Press,
Bury St Edmunds, Suffolk.
Bound by WBC Book Manufacturers Ltd, Bridgend,
Mid-Glamorgan.

T ● To

D J.

Penn

C

AIM BEFORE YOU DRAW

By the same author

Snow on the Sierras
The Trial of Sergeant Cimo
Black Days at Bull Run
Guns of the Pony Express
Wild Riders of Wyoming
Missouri Badman

ONE

It was a night long awaited by the city of New York. Although the fact that pugilism was illegal had precluded advance publicity, it seemed that just about everyone had turned out. The streets leaving to the drinking-place at the corner of Broadway and Howard Street were thronged. It was there, in a basement, doors closed firmly to the police, that the title of American heavyweight champion would be decided. For many the euphoria was muted by the realization that the fight itself would be a brutal life-and-death business. Young Liam Greeley, tough, tremendously strong, pleasingly handsome, was the favourite of just about everyone. But nobody gave him a chance of survival against 'Black' Ketchtom, a veteran of the rough and tumble game that prizefighting was in those days. Ketchtom was not a Negro. The nickname referred to his heart, not the colour of his skin. Politics were also involved. Ketchtom's mentor was Lionel Greenford, a powerful man in the Native American party. With elections on a near horizon, Greenford couldn't afford to have his fighter lose. Greeley's Uncle Elvir, a shameless old boaster to many, a Wild West legend come to town for others, was astute enough, but just as his fighter was seen as no match for Ketchtom, Uncle Elvir was looked upon as no more than fodder for the Greenford political faction to chew up.

None of this, especially 'Black' Ketchtom, worried the supremely self-confident Liam Greeley. He had pickled his hands in brine so that his fists were as hard as hammers. Even so, Uncle Elvir had regularly massaged oil into Greeley's hands. When Uncle Elvir had come to New York from the West to care for the orphaned Liam Greeley, the son of his late sister, he had brought with him a dream that one day the boy would head West and make a name for himself where, unlike in the city, men were real men.

To this end, Uncle Elvir had spent a number of hours every day teaching the infant Liam to fight with fists, a knife, or a gun. Liam Greeley had been handling a six-shooter since when he had been so small that his little arms couldn't lift the weight of it. Now, in a city where guns were only used to shoot a man in the back down a dark alleyway he was a blindingly fast draw and an accurate shot. Uncle Elvir used the oil to safeguard those talents of his protégé while at the same time getting him to his peak as a pugilist. A little wizened by age now, and something like half the size of his nephew, Uncle Elvir was wiry and tough. Liam knew that the old man's tales of having mixed with the hardest of the hard men and the fastest of the gunmen in Kansas, Texas, and God-knows where else, were absolutely true, although scoffed at by the ignorant.

Huge though it was, the basement now appeared to be shrinking as it filled to capacity. There was a reek of alcohol. The air was thickened by cigar smoke, and excitement made voices too loud so that the mass of conversation was painful to the ears.

Greeley could see Ketchtom now. Said to be an Englishman and a former pirate, 'Black' Ketchtom was a fearsome sight to the uninitiated in the pugilistic world. He was at least ten years older than Greeley, and a good six inches taller. But extra height in an opponent was something Greeley welcomed. Although he delivered most of his knock-outs to the jaw, he specialized in body punching. Tutored by Uncle Elvir, Greeley had perfected a turn of his wrist when it was a fraction of an inch from its target. This had his fist twist its way agonizingly deep into an opponent's ribs or gut.

'Look at that man, Liam,' Uncle Elvir said, gesturing with a nod to where Lionel Greenford was talking to Ketchtom, his mouth close to the ear of the fighter. 'What can he tell the poor man when he knows nothing of fisticuffs himself.'

'Calm down, Uncle Elvir,' Greeley advised as dozens of hands reached to touch his shoulders, and mouths silently wished him good luck, the words being whisked away by the general hubbub. 'It's Ketchtom we're fighting, not Greenford.'

'I'd be much happier if that were true,' Uncle Elvir said fervently.

Then a mighty roar bellowed from the crowd. Greeley was moved forward, pushed through people who were saying things to him, trying to shake his hand. But he didn't really see them. They were no more than a blur to him. Then the sight and the sound of them faded completely, and he found himself alone, facing Ketchtom, who wore a grimace on his dark, battered face.

From the moment the fight began, Greeley was thankful that everything his Uncle Elvir said was true. Having taught his nephew fighting skills, body sways, footwork, counter-punching, and feinting, Uncle Elvir had said that Ketchtom had none of these movements. Uncle Elvir had said, and the last few seconds had proved him right, '"Black" Ketchtom is nothing but a bar-room brawler, Liam. With your talent, boy, you can afford to treat him with contempt.'

In the opening exchange, Greeley did exactly that. Pretending to take a wild swing, he deliberately left himself wide open. Believing an early victory had presented itself to him, Ketchtom came in headlong behind a barrage of blows. Swaying to the left from the waist upwards, Greeley evaded the onslaught. Then, before Ketchtom could regain his balance, Greeley stepped in, slamming in corkscrew punches to the body, left and right, left and right. Tortured by the attack to his midriff, Ketchtom attempted to bring himself back into a fighting position, but Greeley's left fist raked across both of his eyes, the hardened knuckles ripping open a criss-crossing of scar tissue.

Partially blinded by his own blood, Ketchtom reeled back. Tuning in to the sights and sounds around him for the first time since the fight had begun, Greeley saw his Uncle Elvir jumping up and down with excitement, shouting orders that were drowned out by the shouts of the crowd as the agile Greeley leapt forwards. Left fist pumping out in front of him, he pounded Ketchtom's already bloodied face. But the old campaigner was far from beaten. Ketchtom threw a looping right hand that hit Greeley thuddingly on the side of the neck. Knocking him sideways, it all but felled him. Moving fast while Greeley was struggling to recover, Ketchtom caught the younger man with another looping right. This time it was further up, landing heavily on the side of Greeley's head, the knuckles of Ketchtom's fist pounding Greeley's ear.

Reminded of just how dangerous his opponent was, Greeley shook his head to clear it. Then he resumed command of the fight. Three slashing left hands opened up more old cuts around Ketchtom's eyes, and he staggered back.

There was the roar of the crowd now, which was for Greeley what liquor is to an alcoholic. Loving it, he put his punches rhythmically together so that his fists beat a constant tattoo on Ketchtom's head and body. Greeley caught sight of Greenford, grim-faced and silent, although one of his confederates at his side, a small man with a broken nose, was shouting angrily at Ketchtom, advising him on how to deal with Greeley's attack.

The toughness of Ketchtom kept the fight going for fifty-three minutes. Neither was the battle completely one-sided, for Greeley was occasionally caught by hard blows that had his senses reeling. But then he saw his chance. As Ketchtom raised both hands in a desperate attempt to rub away the blood that filled his eyes, Greeley moved smartly forward. The right hand he delivered to his opponent's belly seemed to sink in to the elbow. Ready for the head of Ketchtom to come forward, Greeley measured the distance with a pawing left hand, then released a dynamite right hand to the jaw.

Face a bloodied pulp, his ribcage a mass of blue, black and red contusions, Ketchtom staggered back into the crowd. Lionel Greenford, distaste showing on his face, grabbed his bleeding fighter and supported him. The man with the broken nose was yelling instructions at an exceptionally thin, tall man, who produced a bottle of liquor and held it to the battered mouth of Ketchtom, Greeley was aware of Uncle Elvir shouting his objections, complaining that the pugilist should be pushed back into the ring at once.

Everything happened so quickly then that it was such a blur that no one could later claim to have the events in order. It seemed to Greeley that as his Uncle Elvir's protests gained fury, so did the man with the broken nose produce a gun. Uncle Elvir went into a crouch, bringing up a gun and firing it in one smooth motion. The bullet went past broken-nose to nick off the top of the tall man's right ear. Blood spurted upwards from the ruined ear; a sight that seemed to fascinate everyone. But then Uncle Elvir staggered backwards, colliding with Greeley before slumping to the floor, a growing dark red stain on his shirt-front and vest.

Greeley had time to see the smoking gun in the hand of the man with the broken nose, before panic hit the crowd. Already breaking the law by attending the fight, they were sure that the shot would bring the police, and there was a mass exodus that turned into a swarming, punching, kicking and biting bottle-neck by the door.

Scooping to pick up his Uncle Elvir, Greeley felt a hand on his arm and heard the voice of a friend. 'Bring him this way, Liam.'

Going out of a side door, ringed by a handful of supporters, Greeley carried his unconscious, bleeding uncle to a cart that someone had commandeered as an ambulance. Laying Uncle Elvir in the bed of the cart, a distraught Greeley could see that he was in a bad way. The horse was moved off, pulling the cart at a walking pace so as not to jar the badly injured man. Including Greeley, the escort around the improvised ambulance numbered seven.

'We'll get him to the hospital,' one of the men said superfluously.

'As quickly as possible,' another voice said, frightened after having taken a look at the bleeding old man in the cart.

The hour was late, the streets deserted except for the little party with the cart. Greeley could feel the sweat chilling on his body in the cold night air. The differing temperature from inside the drinking place had a short, rotund man show concern. 'Elvir will be in shock. He needs to be kept warm, hold up there now.'

As the cart stopped, so did the fat man rip off his coat, saying, 'Let's have your coats, boys, and we'll cover Elvir.'

Everyone but Greeley, who was bare to the waist, took off their coats. Fussing over the stricken Uncle Elvir, the short man covered him, layer after layer, tucking the old man in as if he was a child in a cot. They had paused on the corner of Broadway and

Anthony Street, and were about to move off when the night erupted into violence around them.

An angry mob spilled out of the Bella Union. They were Lionel Greenford's supporters, and they came at the group around the cart, smashing at them, pushing them out of the way. Determined to save his uncle, Greeley downed three men with his fists and crippled two by kicking them. But there were too many.

Hands had hold of the cart, rocking it, causing the still unconscious Uncle Elvir to roll from side to side, and the horse to shriek out in fright, adding to the pandemonium.

At the moment that the cart was about to be capsized, help came from the Fifth Precinct station-house. Wielding long clubs the police came out. Descending on the mob, they cracked heads, clearing a way to the cart by felling bodies left right and centre.

'Are yeeze heading for the hospital?' a tall cop with an Irish accent asked Greeley, having taken a look at the cart and Uncle Elvir.

'We are,' Greeley confirmed, relieved to have been saved from the mob.

'Then by the look of your man, you'd better make it fast,' the policeman advised.

They set the horse into a trot then, with policemen jogging at their side until they got to the New York Hospital. Two policemen carried Uncle Elvir in, with Greeley hurrying after them, having assured his helpers that they could leave and he would keep them informed of Uncle Elvir's condition.

They took Uncle Elvis into a room, where doctors and nurses, their faces serious, crowded in after them. The two policemen came out to stand with a shivering Greeley in a drab, depressing corridor. Reaching for his face, holding his chin in a forefinger and thumb, turning his head this way and that to survey him from all angles, the Irish cop told Greeley, 'Sure, we'll see the old man fixed up first, spalpeen, then we'll be needing to talk to you about your carryings-on this evening.'

In other circumstances Greeley would have been alarmed at the prospect of being arrested for prizefighting, but now Uncle Elvir was all that mattered to him. The two policeman were sympathetic and tried to be friendly, but the time passed with an intolerable slowness.

At last the doctors and nurses came out of the room, all but one of them going the other way. It was a woman who came to Greeley, her strange uniform making her as frightening as a ghost in the night for him. Her age-lined face and manner told Greeley that she held a senior position in the hospital.

'He wants to speak to you now,' she said, her expression causing him to anticipate a smile that never materialized.

'Thank God,' Greeley breathed out the two words in relief as he walked at the side of the woman. He had feared that Uncle Elvir would never regain consciousness, never speak to him again.

When they reached the door and the elderly nurse put a hand on his arm to stop him, indicating that she wouldn't be coming with him, Greeley was giving her a grateful smile when her words turned his heart to stone.

'Go into him now, son. Be ready to say goodbye.'

Uncle Elvir was lying flat on a bed, his face whiter than the single sheet that covered him. Remembering what the man in the street had said about cold and shock, Greeley was momentarily angry with the hospital staff for not wrapping the old man in blankets. The dying deserved a bit of comfort as they crossed over, surely. But then he found that it was warm in the room. They hadn't neglected his beloved Uncle Elvir.

When he got to the bed the eyelids were closed in the waxen face, and Greeley feared that he was too late. But he detected a flickering of the lids. They lifted, going only a little over halfway up, and only the eyes turned to him, the head lying still because the old man lacked both the strength and energy to move it. The lips that had told Greeley so many tales, had given him so much invaluable advice, moved this way and that several times before Uncle Elvir could speak. When he did the faint, gasping voice bore no relation to the raucous tones of the old, often verbose, Uncle Elvir.

'You know what you have to do now, boy.'

Not understanding, Greeley nodded assent to humour the hurt old man. But some of the old Uncle Elvir fire remained, and he managed to turn his head slightly in Greeley's direction to scold him.

'I may have a hole in my chest, Liam, but there's still brain in my head, boy. Now stop your silly head-nodding and listen to me. You're on your own now, but I've prepared you for it.'

'I've still got you, Uncle Elvir,' Greeley said in an effort at reassuring himself more than anything.

'We don't have time to spout nonsense, Liam,' the old man's voice gained strength from somewhere. 'Leave this God-forsaken city, boy. Go out West and make your mark. I won't be dead, Liam, because you can live out there for the both of us if you do it right. Promise me that you'll make something of yourself out there.'

The once deft, fast-moving old hand slid off the bed to clasp Greeley's hand. Greeley was shocked to find how cold were the fingers as Uncle Elvir, his voice no more than a whisper, said. 'This is it, Liam, son. I can call you that now because I have always regarded you as my boy.'

'You've been more than a father to me, Uncle Elvir.'

'You earned that Liam, because you are a really special man. What you possess can be used in two ways, so make sure that you always pause to check you have made the right choice.'

Wanting to question the old man as to what he meant, Greeley held back, his eyes brimming with tears as he saw how rapidly his uncle was sinking. The eyes had closed again and the voice was close to being indistinct as it reached Greeley, who bent forward to catch the words.

'Of all the things I've taught you, son, remember that the most important is – aim before you draw.'

Uncle Elvir died then. Clasping the hand in both of his, Greeley dropped to his knees beside the bed, wanting to pray but failing, because that was something his uncle had never taught him. So his sobbing became his praying, and he didn't know how long he had been kneeling there when a voice said quietly from the doorway, 'Come, lad, let's be having you.'

It was the big Irish cop, and Greeley turned away, wiping at his eyes with a palm of his hand, ashamed to be seen crying. Getting to his feet, he took slow, dragging paces across the room. At the door he turned to take his last look at Uncle Elvir, then stepped out into the corridor.

Both of the policemen were waiting, standing close, not intending to lose him. But they were standing on the threshold of Greeley's new life. They would, for a considerable time when they got him into court, delay the journey west that Uncle Elvir had asked him to make. It was a deathbed request that Greeley had answered with a promise.

'I'm sorry for your trouble, lad,' the big Irish cop said from the heart. He was standing facing Greeley, while the other policeman was standing at Greeley's right shoulder, ready to place an arresting hand on his arm.

Greeley exploded into action. Swinging his right arm out, he caught the policeman at his side a heavy backhanded blow across the face. The Irish policeman came forward, but Greeley moved too fast for him.

Seeing that the second policeman was reeling from the blow, but still on his feet, Greeley sank his right hand into the soft belly of the lawman, then flattened him with a vicious right hand to the head. Escaping the clutching fingers of the Irishman by less than an inch. Greeley ran off down the corridor.

There were screams as he charged through a ward in which alarmed patients sat up in bed as he passed. Greeley crashed against a table, sending something made of glass to smash on the floor, the sound generating more screaming. As he went through the door at the end of the ward, he collided with a man, no more than a silhouette that smelled of antiseptic and grunted a foul oath in a gruff voice as it crashed to the ground.

In another corridor, Greeley ran up to a glass-panelled door that showed that the welcoming night and freedom was just outside. Behind him he could hear the heavy plodding of the Irish cop's feet. The door was locked. Standing back, Greeley delivered a hard kick that shattered the lock and had the glass disintegrate to fall noisily about him.

Then he was out in the night, running, following a wide path that logic told him must lead to a gate in the rail-enclosed hospital grounds. There was still the sound of a one-man pursuit behind him. Having seen what Greeley had done to his partner with his fists, the Irish policeman would already be swinging his club in anticipation. Having in mind the size of the fellow, and the size of the stick that he carried, Greeley knew that his chances of freedom would be in jeopardy, to say the very least, if the Irish cop got within striking distance of him.

Puffing hard now, despite being superbly fit, Greeley reached the gate and pulled at it. The iron framework wouldn't budge. He tried again, able to hear the Irishman's laboured breathing now as well as his footfalls. The gate refused to open, and Greeley experienced despair as his exploring fingers found the padlock and chain. The hospital was secured overnight. He would meet the same whichever gate he went to.

Turning, his back to the gate, he saw the policeman loom up out of the darkness, his club raised in readiness as he called, 'Stand still now, lad. There's no need for anyone else to be hurted if ye're sensible.'

Swinging round to face the gate, Greeley grasped the upright bars and pulled himself up. It was an awkward, scrambling exercise, and he felt the wind of the policeman's club, and heard it clang against the gate just below his feet, before he somehow made it to the top. There were sharp spikes there, intended to deter intruders, but just as dangerous to an escapee like Greeley. Not sure what he was doing in the dark, he bent over to clutch at two spikes while he stood on two others, the points digging into the soles of his shoes. Standing upright, balancing like a performer in a circus, he took a deep breath and launched himself into the unknown of utter darkness.

Greeley went down and down, beginning to worry. But then he landed on solid ground, making his knees into shock absorbers by bending them springingly. No sooner had his feet touched ground than he was running. Free, delightfully, wonderfully free, he heard the Irish cop yelling through the bars of the gate at him. Expecting threats and anger, an astonished Greeley heard encouragement.

'God speed, lad,' the Irishman was shouting. 'Keep running, and may God bless you.'

With these unexpected good wishes ringing in disbelieving ears, Greeley didn't slacken his pace. A plan was taking shape in his head now. When he made a start it would be from scratch. Apart from one single dime in his pocket he had no money. Due to the interruption he hadn't been paid for fighting that evening, and what he had earned in the past his Uncle Elvir had looked after for him. It would be tough in the immediate future, but he found himself relishing the challenge.

But first he had obligations to his girlfriend of long standing – the lovely Martha Jane Ackerman. Keeping to the backstreets, far away from club-swinging cops who could well be on the look-out for a pugilist still stripped to the waist.

In this way he reached the alley that ran behind the row of terraced houses, in one of which the Ackerman family lived. By feel in the dark, he counted the number of tall wooden gates in the high brick-built back wall that ran behind the houses. A mistake could land him in big trouble.

Satisfied that he had the right house, he pulled himself up to the top of the wall. Balancing there, he could just make out the wall that ran along to the projecting tenement that was Martha Jane's room. As surefooted as a cat he went along the top of the wall until he came to the house. Holding on with his right hand he reached to the window with his left. His fingers were a good yard from the edge of the window, and there was nothing to support him to go across. Although feeling that it was tempting fate to get rid of it, Greeley took his last dime from his pocket. Taking careful aim, he tossed the coin at the window.

He heard it hit the glass, but there was no response. Greeley was trying to decide on his next move, but no ideas presented themselves, when he was relieved to see the closed curtain of the window lifted back a little. Waving an arm, he wanted to somehow reassure Martha Jane, but knew that it was hopeless because she couldn't see him in the dark. Then the curtain went back down into place, and his heart fell with it.

There was no more time to waste. He had to make his way through the city of New York before dawn came to expose the furtive and the nefarious on the streets. It hurt him not to bid Martha Jane farewell, but he would get in touch with her as soon as possible.

Greeley had taken three careful paces back along the wall when he heard the sash of the window behind him being raised. Arms out, he did a tight-rope walker's turn and called softly, 'Martha Jane.'

First her black-haired head and then her shoulders came out through the window into the night. 'Is it you, Liam Greeley?'

'It is,' he replied, as if introducing himself at the front door and not balancing on a yard-dividing wall.

'You're an awful fool, Liam,' she protested, thinking he was playing one of his pranks to see the girl that he loved. Then she blinked as her eyes became accustomed to the darkness. 'You've no shirt or coat. You'll catch your death of cold, Liam. What are you up to?'

'Something's happened,' he told her, and he found that emotion caused his voice to crack, making it too loud in the circumstances, as he added, 'Uncle Elvir is dead.'

'Oh, heaven forbid,' the girl cried in a low voice.

'I have to leave New York, Martha Jane.'

'Why?' she enquired. 'Where will you go?'

'I'm going out West,' he told her, answering her second question, ignoring her first.

Martha Jane gave a little sob that was more a catch in her throat. 'You can't leave me, Liam.'

'It will be only for a short while. I'll send for you as soon as I'm settled.'

'You promise?'

'I swear it.'

It sounded good, but Greeley had a sudden cold feeling. Here they were, lovers who couldn't even touch when they said goodbye. Was the unbridgeable gap between them right now symbolic of something that would keep them apart in the future?

'Could you get me one of your father's shirts?'

As he called this, the tension of the whole evening built to a pitch in Greeley. Asking the girl to steal a shirt for him was a reminder of a line from a familiar song about a soldier promising to marry his sweetheart. Greeley suddenly had a compelling urge to laugh, but he knew that if he gave way to it the incipient chuckle would lead to hysterical laughter.

Never one to question anyone who needed help, him in particular, Martha Jane went from the window. Then she was back, saying. 'All I could get was a coat. Catch!'

She tossed the garment and he had to lean precariously out to his left, arm extended fully. The jacket passed by, too far away from him, but then the cuff of one sleeve brushed his fingers and he grabbed it. Greeley was so off balance stretching to catch the jacket that the weight of it almost pulled him from the wall. Countering by swinging the jacket round and round in the air by the sleeve, he saved himself.

'Thank you, Martha Jane,' he said from the bottom of his heart.

'I will come and find you if you don't send for me, Liam Greeley,' she warned.

'You won't have to do that,' he promised. 'I want you with me as soon as possible.'

'And I want to be with you,' she whispered.

'I must go now, Martha Jane. If we don't say goodbye it will be easier for us to say hello when we meet again.'

With that he turned, and without a word, but with a wave of his hand that she couldn't see in the darkness, he started off along the wall in the direction of the alley. As he was preparing to jump down he thought he heard her call something to him softly. Unable to be sure that he had heard it, and because it was impossible to answer her if she had, he dropped down into the alley.

From then on the blackness of the night was his friend, shielding him, hiding him from the eyes of suspicious policemen who lurked in the most unexpected places in a rough and tough city.

Liam Greeley didn't run, but he walked fast with the steady stride of a man who knows exactly where he is going. His destination was the railway yards at Jamestown.

TWO

There were four of them altogether hiding in the dark recesses of a closed but empty box car, conversing in whispers. Greeley still couldn't impress on himself that the three other men were below him because they were tramps. All four of them were penniless and homeless, he sported a stubbly beard now as they did, and the upper part of his body was clad only in a jacket. Having learned the rule of the road that everyone went under an assumed name, he had chosen New York Joe for himself. Only the last name was ever used in conversation, and he was 'Joe' to his fellow travellers. One, a chubby fellow despite constantly whining that he 'hadn't had a bite for days,' was Peoria Fatty. Another was a young kid who coughed a lot and looked too delicate to be riding the rods. He was identified not by his place of origin, but by his former occupation, which made him Waiter George. The third man was elderly. Known as Illinois Dago, he was paid the deference and respect that hoboes paid to any of their number whose hair had turned to grey.

It was Dago who whispered now as the freight train gave a shudder. 'She is off, boys. We'll be at Clarksburg in time to hustle a hot supper.'

Barely had the old tramp got his words out than the large door was jerked open and a tough-looking brakeman, complete with a heavy stick, stood peering into the darkness.

Catching sight of them, the brakeman pulled his considerable bulk up into the car. More shuddering and some hesitant movement of the train made Fatty say philosophically. 'Methinks we are about to be invited to leave this side-door Pullman.'

'Hit the grit, you hoboes, and be quick about it,' the brakeman ordered in a scratched-throat voice, unafraid although he was one against four. 'This ain't no accommodation train for bums and deadheads.'

Seeing his companions ready to comply, Greeley copied them. Since making his way West he had worked on the principle that the tramps knew the business far better than he did, so he was guided by them. Fatty jumped out of the box car first, Greeley followed, and George came behind him. They were out by the water tank which was the reason for the halt in the first place. Being thrown off out in the wilds like this, Greeley had learned, was something the hoboes went to great lengths to avoid.

The train was already moving, but Dago sat in the doorway of the car, legs dangling as he addressed the trainman. 'You, my good sir, would seem to lack the love of one's neighbour as preached by our Lord Jesus Christ.'

To Greeley's knowledge, the old tramp had no interest whatsoever in religion, and he guessed that Dago was playing a game, putting some ploy into play as the train gained speed.

'Hit the dirt,' the brakeman yelled at the hobo, casting an anxious glance at a train that was now moving fairly fast. Raising his stick, he went towards Dago, yelling, 'Hit the grit!'

Determined to protect the old tramp, Greeley grabbed the wrist of the arm the trainman had raised with the stick, and dug his fingers in hard. To his amazement,

Fatty and George ran past him and the brakeman and jumped back up into the box car. Dago pulled his legs in, and they closed the door with a bang.

Jerking his arm free, the brakeman spat scornful words at Greeley. 'You're a right wise guy! How long you been on the road, bo? I wasn't going to hit him.' He pointed at the fast receding box car. 'Now look wot you done.'

Scowling at Greeley, the brakeman waited until the tail end of the train with the caboose passed at speed, then swung expertly up on to its rear platform.

Waving his clenched fist back at Greeley, he shouted. 'I'll get them bums at the next stop. As for you, you're stuck. Nixie place this! Nixie place this! Nothing stops here!'

Greeley stood watching the train become distant, diminishing in size until it disappeared from his life. Still somehow caught in the air and held there were the brakeman's triumphant words, 'Nixie place this!'

Three hours later, having sat under the water tank vainly hoping for a train upon which to ramble further West, Greeley learned why it was such a bad place. The news came from a track walker who appeared along the line at a steady lope, a hammer on his shoulder. He looked at Greeley through eyes that were deepset in a face that had been leathered by the elements.

'Reckon as how you got a mighty long wait setting there, mister?'

'How do you see that?' Greeley asked, standing to ease out his legs, stretching his arms above his head and yawning.

Staying on the move, ready to pass the time of day with a hobo but no more, the trackman said. 'It's real rare that trains ever stop to take water from this tank. You could be waiting days, feller, maybe weeks. There's a junction yonder,' he pointed north-west, 'where every train do stop at a coal chute for a supply of coal.'

'How far?'

'Thirty mile. Just one homestead along the way, Jem Master's place,' the track walker said as he walked away, leaving Greeley achingly hungry and morbidly miserable.

It had been breakfast of the previous day that he had last eaten. That had been at a large hobo camp-fire. As always with outsiders, Greeley had been ostracized by the tramps who had moved away to light a fire separate from the one he sat at. Illinois Dago had pleaded his case, and he had at last been taken into the tramp fold. This had all been so long ago that his stomach had forgotten.

Faced with no other choice than a long walk, he set off. Soon wearying, feeling weak from hunger, he looked all the time for a change in the barren landscape, but there was none, despite the trackman's assurance that a homestead lay along the way. Greeley had passed the eighteenth mile-post from the water tank before he saw the welcome sight of a typical low building of a Western homestead. It lay in a slight depression a short distance from the right-of-way he had been following.

Turning off towards the house, Greeley's hopes faded as he saw several well-worn paths plainly showing that every tramp forced to walk from the water tank had tried his luck here. With prospects already grim, he saw bad news chalked on the trunk of a small half-dead tree in the form of a circle with a cross inside. It was the hoboes' sign warning that 'The people living here don't give.'

Doubting that he could cover the remainder of the trek to the railway junction without food, Greeley had to give it a try. He went in through a dilapidated gate into a yard surrounding a roughly-built residence. Catching sight of a broken go-cart and some dolls lying around, Greeley called on his short apprenticeship on the road to conjure up a story that might bring the best results.

He had not reached the house when a young woman, buxom and with a prettiness that shouldn't be hidden away out in the wilds, stepped out from the porch and in no uncertain tone of voice addressed him. 'Well, sir, and what might you be looking for?'

Asking neither for food nor drink, Greeley humbly requested that he be permitted to rest awhile. Had they been there, then Peoria Fatty and Illinois Dago would have been proud of him. He read the confusion in the woman's frowning eyes. Puzzled, she commented. 'All the other travellers always beg for grub, but Jem, my husband, has given me strict orders not to feed any tramps, and I am mighty pleased to see one "gentleman" among all those who have passed this place since we homesteaded it.'

Easing himself down tiredly to sit on the stump of a tree that was scarred by years of firewood being sliced on it, Greeley, who had learned fast and well from his erstwhile tramp companions, explained, 'I am not a tramp, ma'am, but a man down on his luck. I lost my work through no fault of my own, and now I'm looking for employment to support my wife and children. My old mommy and daddy look to me for support, too. Last night I had my shirt and wallet stolen while I slept. My money and rail ticket was taken, so the conductor turned me off the passenger at the water tank.'

Close to fainting from lack of food, he looked her squarely in the eyes. After a few minutes' silence he was rewarded by the flitting of a sympathetic expression across her face, then she said, curtly so as not to encourage him too much. 'I reckon as how I can give you a snack or something, stranger, seeing as how you're a married man and as such will know how to behave himself. You're in a right fix by the sound of it, so you better come in and rest while I heat you up a cup of coffee.'

The house he was invited into was a two-room affair, one the sleeping-room and the other the parlour, dining-room and kitchen combined. A girl aged about seven peered shyly round a corner at him, then vanished. The woman made him sit in a rocking chair, and he had to fight sleep that instantly tried to overpower him because he was so comfortable.

'How old are your parents?' she asked, her tone suggesting to him that she wanted to make some comparison with an experience of her own.

Not wanting to overdo it, he diluted what the tramps he had been with would have said. Even then it sounded a bit too much once he had put it into words. 'My father is ninety-two, but he gets along pretty well, being as his eyes are letting him down more and more each day. Mother's quite a bit younger, eighty-six, but she's stone deaf, which makes for problems all round.'

The woman nodded. Her reddish hair would have been real nice if cared for properly. Not that it didn't add to her attraction right then. She had filled a mug of coffee for him, and he knew that he had won with his imaginary aged parents when after a moment's hesitation, she asked. 'Do you like fried eggs?'

Greeley could do nothing but nod because his stomach was twisting at his throat, strangling him in anticipation as she cracked six huge eggs into a large pan and the sizzling and the aroma was almost too much for him to bear. One of her strong brown hands held a loaf she had baked, while the other sawed off two huge chunks of bread. Wondering where the man of the house was, Greeley feared that he might return at any moment and end this dream.

But there were no interruptions. Motioning him up to the table, she spread butter thickly on the bread as he sat and pulled the plate of eggs towards him. Not wanting to let himself down by bolting the food, he was so starved that he ate ravenously, listening to her saying something, but enjoying the meal too much to decipher her words.

When the last scrap was gone from his plate, and he wiped it clean with what remained of the bread, wolfing it down, she gave him a smile with a good set of teeth. 'There's a lot of satisfaction for a woman in watching a man enjoy his food.'

A clattering made by something falling came from the other room. Then he could hear the girl softly singing a hymn. She gave a giggle of embarrassment and went silent.

The woman stood and went into the sleeping-room. There was a low buzz of conversation between mother and daughter. When the woman returned she was carrying a blue shirt, which she handed to him. 'That may be a mite tight for you, but it will fit, I'm sure of that.'

'Well, thank you, ma'am,' he said, standing, wanting to get away to ride the first available train, needing desperately to escape from the kindness he had provoked with his lies.

'You don't know my name,' she said, lowering her good-looking head a little, as coy now as her little girl had been when she had peeped at Greeley. 'It's Norah,' she added, just as if they were a girl and boy meeting at a church social back in New York.

A warning siren blared inside of Greeley's head. Having quickly adapted to his enforced new way of life, he could handle the toughest tramp at a fire, and was totally unafraid of the largest and most belligerent railwaymen, but this was different.

'It's a very lonely life out here,' she said.

Standing close to him now, she was perfumed by the cooking she had just done for him, but the natural scent of woman was there too, and Greeley was most conscious of this. But he knew he had to head for the door. There was Martha Jane back in New York, a little girl in the next room, and an unsuspecting husband going about his chores somewhere.

Snatching up the shirt, he blurted, 'I'm grateful to you for the meal and the shirt, ma'am, it was mighty kind of you.'

Going out through the door he headed at a half run for the right-of-way that would take him, now fortified with food and coffee, to the coal chute and the next train West. Behind him he heard her call out something, but he neither listened nor turned his head. As he started to tread the worn right-of-way, he heard her shout. There was a mournful kind of wail to her voice, but he was now too distant to catch her words if he tried. Greeley hurried on, feeling terribly guilty, but uncertain as to where the guilt he felt belonged.

It was dusk by the time he reached the junction, making it easier for him to approach the westbound train that was taking in a supply of coal. He passed just one tramp, who greeted him and asked the almost obligatory question of those who travelled the roads. 'Ho, bo, which way?'

'West,' Greeley gave his direction, following the code with his own question. 'Which way you, bo?'

'East, bo. Jamestown, New York.'

This caused Greeley a smile as he moved furtively along the stationary train. It was a strange world, with the departure place of one man being the destination of another.

He pulled into the shadows between cars while two engineers went by, too engrossed in conversation to notice him. Then he tried doors, found one open and swung up into the car, closing the door behind him. It was a refrigerator car, but it would have to do. They were top-heavy, especially those in which dressed beef-halves were hung, and they made an uncomfortable ride. An advantage was that this type of car made it hazardous for the train crew to walk over the roofs while the train was in motion. It was far more unpleasant and dangerous for any hobo foolish enough, or desperate enough, to ride underneath the bottom of one of the rocking and swaying cars of this class. Putting on the shirt given him by the obliging homesteader's wife, Greeley put his coat back on top, turned up the collar, wrapped his arms around himself and settled down. Although he still had no money, he told himself optimistically that things must be improving as he had gained a shirt since leaving New York.

Cold but secure, Greeley journeyed to Meadowville. Opening the door and dropping to the ground, body stiff and uncooperative at first, he walked through the large depot, knowing that he must seek out the Kansas Pacific Railroad for the final leg of his journey West. In that special darkness that says midnight has passed, a call came to him from the shadows cast by two barely separated buildings.

'Ho, bo.'

Recognizing the guarded, whispering call as that of a tramp, Greeley returned. 'Ho, bo, what gives?'

Small, carrying a bundle tied to a stick on its shoulder, a figure slid out to come up to Greeley and identify itself. 'Chicago Jimmy, bo.'

'New York Joe.'

'Tread carefully, Joe,' Jimmy warned, 'this place is strictly hostile. There's a paid watchman by the name of Spitz, and he's a hobo killer.'

Moving off, Greeley found that Chicago Jimmy was going with him. Having learned to prefer being a loner since leaving New York, Greeley found that there was an odd comfort in having Jimmy with him. He guessed that he was using the tramp as a replacement for the once ever-present Uncle Elvir.

'This Spitz would nick his father's picture if he found it riding deadhead on a train . . .' Chicago Jimmy was saying when two huge hands came out of the darkness, one grabbing Jimmy's shoulder, the other clamping vice-like on Greeley, the powerful fingers digging in painfully and deep.

'What are you deadheads doing in the depot this time of night?' a deep voice rumbled the question out at them.

Greeley prepared himself to attack. The hand holding him was outsized, but its owner would be no match for Greeley. After all, if it hadn't been for the unfortunate set of incidents that had led to the tragic death of Uncle Elvir, Greeley would right now be the American heavyweight pugilistic champion.

Chicago Jimmy read his mind. 'No, Joe, don't do it. This is Spitz, and you don't know Meadowville. Take a swing at him and they'll have you hanging from a gibbet at dawn.'

Greeley took the advice and the two of them were led into town to a lock-up. A sheriff, well past his prime of life and with a face and eyes pleading for sleep, listened tiredly to Spitz's report of the arrest, wrote something in a book, then slammed Chicago Jimmy and Greeley securely into a cell.

Spitz looked gloatingly in at them before he left, telling them, 'The Judge in this here town ain't never given no deadhead less than nine months in the hoosegow for hoboing.'

Having been warned by other men of the road that there were hobo-hating towns, Greeley believed the watchman, although it saddened him greatly to do so. Certain that a prosperous future was awaiting him in the West, he fretted at it being delayed for close to a year by a jail sentence. Then there was Martha Jane. Waiting to hear from him, she'd think he had abandoned her when she received no word.

In the morning a sour-faced deputy poked a dry ham sandwich through the bars at each of them. Taking no chances, he gave them both an empty enamel mug, then filled it from a jug at a cautious arm's length.

'When's the judge sit?' Jimmy enquired.

'You two'll be up before him in two hours,' the deputy said like he was talking to a couple of stray curs.

'At least we ain't going to be kept waiting to learn our fate,' a philosophical Chicago Jimmy commented to a disconsolate Liam Greeley.

An hour later there came the sounds of general mayhem from out in the town. There was shouting, gunshots, and then some screaming. More shouting was followed by additional screaming, then another, single gunshot that sounded close.

Greeley and Jimmy pressed against the bars for a better view of the jail as the door burst open. The sheriff with the over-tired look came in with a gun drawn, covering three tough-looking prisoners wearing duster coats. One of the prisoners was holding an arm that bled from a gunshot wound, and two of the three deputies behind the sheriff carried the deputy who had fed Greeley and Jimmy that morning. The sour face was ashen, and the amount of blood soaking the injured deputy's shirt suggested to Greeley that he was dead.

'A bank raid,' Chicago Jimmy breathed out in awe as the sheriff came over and unlocked the door of their steel cage.

'Vamoose, you two, quick as you like,' the sheriff grunted at the surprised pair of captives.

Not needing to be told twice, they jumped from the cage as the sheriff and deputies, having caught bigger fish than a couple of no-account hoboes, pushed the bank robbers roughly into the cage.

As they went, heading for the rail depot at a fast walk, not wanting to attract attention by running, Chicago Jimmy warned. 'We still gotta watch out for Spitz. He'll kill us with his bare hands rather than see us go free.'

When they were among the trains they found that the excitement in town had drawn most railwaymen away. But they still needed to be cautious, and Chicago Jimmy asked the usual opening question in what was to be the closing of his brief relationship with Greeley. 'Which way, bo?'

'West, Jimmy, West,' Greeley replied, liking the sound of his planned destination. 'Which way for you, boy'

'East,' Chicago Jimmy said with a determination to show that he couldn't be persuaded otherwise. About to walk away, he stepped closer to Greeley, asking, 'Summat tells me you ain't been on the road all that long, Joe, is that right?'

'You've got it,' Greeley was ready to admit.

'Then you needs a bit of advice, bo. Don't try to ride out of here in a car. You do, and Spitz or some of his buddies will get you, sure as shootin'. You learned how to ride the rods?'

'Not yet.'

'Then I'll show you before we part, bo,' Chicago Jimmy said, leading the way to a stationary Kansas Pacific Railroad train.

Ducking under a freight car, Jimmy signalled for Greeley to do the same, then pointed up underneath to where a couple of thin iron rods upheld the body of the car. 'Stretch yourself across them, bo.'

Showing Greeley how to straddle the thin iron rods, Chicago Jimmy had his doubts whether the big young man fully realized the sort of ride that was ahead of him. 'You got a bandanna, bo?'

'Yep,' Greeley said, pulling a large yellow neckerchief from his pocket.

'Then tie it over your nose and mouth, Joe, to keep out the dust. That's the only protection you're going to have. Most of us wear thick overalls, heavy gauntlets and gloves when we ride the rods. Tain't no fun, bo.

Far from it, bo.'

Chicago Jimmy had never said a truer word. As the train eased away, so did Greeley consider that his temporary tramping friend had exaggerated. His position couldn't be described as comfortable, but nothing more was required than to keep a steady but light grip with hands and feet. But when the train gained speed he had a rapid change of mind. Greeley had to cling on for dear life as the car careered along, jolting, bouncing, rocking, while the whirling, whirring wheels added to the bedlam by whining and screeching on every curve. All the time he was bombarded not only by flying dust, but by sand, cinders, pebbles and good sized rocks which the speeding train forced through the air like shots from a gun.

The ride went on for what Greeley estimated must have been seventy miles. The skin of his face was peppered and he knew that his clothing must be in a mess. A respite came as the train slowed to tackle a steep up-grade. Peering out from his precarious perch under the wagon, Greeley recognized, from descriptions given him, the treeless banks of the Smoky Hill River. The town in which he had chosen to make a start, Oaksworth, could lie at the top of this gradient, or it might yet be many miles ahead. Whatever, Greeley's body was refusing to ride the rods any longer.

Timing the move well, encouraged by the slow speed of the train, he released his grip. Landing on his back jarringly against the sleepers, he rolled to his left, coming out safely between the wheels and continuing to roll down a bank.

First kneeling, Greeley then stood on feet so numb that they couldn't tell him that they were in contact with the ground. Initially in a falling-step walk he headed to where he could hear the gentle movement of the river. Life came back into his limbs, and he was walking proud and upright in his pugilist's style when he got to the river's edge and knelt to put both of his hot, cinder-scarred hands into the cooling, healing water.

Greeley next bathed his face. Then he used a clump of moss as a makeshift sponge to clean his jacket down. Then he washed the shirt given him by the woman at the homestead. Laying it out in the sun to dry, he stretched his body out on the grassy bank and rested.

An hour later, after a nap that refreshed him, Greeley stood up and got dressed. As smart and presentable as any penniless man in his position could be, and very hungry again now, he began walking. He followed in the direction the train had taken, knowing that, sooner or later, he would reach the town of Oaksworth.

THREE

Liam Greeley thought it fitting that Oaksworth was a town in an embryonic stage. It seemed just the right place for a man like himself who was about to be born again. Lying flat on the banks of Smoky Hill River, it was surrounded by an infinite prairie of grama grass. As a cattle-shipping point it hadn't progressed past receiving just a few herds yet, but the potential was there, and those who ran honky-tonks and gambling dives had moved into town, very aware of the prospects. Made up of four blocks of frame structures, the main street ran parallel with the railroad tracks. The new Santa Fe Railroad had cast a covetous eye on Oaksworth, but the Kansas Pacific had got in first by making considerable investment in the town. Surveyors for the railroad were working on the establishment of a new cattle trail that would lead into the loading pens at Oaksworth. Powerful advertising by the Kansas Pacific was spreading the news about Oaksworth throughout ranching country.

Enthralled, the recently arrived Greeley stood breathing in the smells of Oaksworth. The odour of new pine lumber in the hastily erected buildings of Main Street was pungent. Perhaps it was a stench that came from excited Texas cattle crammed into the shipping yards, but it was a headier scent to Greeley as he stood and silently revelled in the yells of the cowhands, the continuous bawling of cattle, and the dust-muted drumming of horses' hooves.

There was a good feel to the place. It felt like his town as he looked into a dark red sundown that he regarded as marking the death of his old life. Tomorrow the new would begin, but he knew that he could not endure his hunger until then, neither did he intend to sleep with the rats under some raised building that night.

A crippled young man, holding his right arm up tight against his chest like a bird with a broken wing, strolled up to stand close as Greeley watched sections of a wooden building being unloaded from railroad cars.

'That's Richmond Coles's place, the American Playground, being shipped in from Abilene,' the disabled youngster volunteered.

Having seen other saloons on Main Street, Pat Brogan's, the Cattleman's Cottage, and others the names of which he couldn't bring to mind, all of them sizeable places, Greeley was astonished that a saloon could be transported in that way. A well-built young man in expensive clothes, a felt hat tilted to the back of his head, supervised the unloading from a distance that protected him and his clothing. Even before the crippled boy had identified the man for him, Greeley had assumed that it was Richmond Coles, the owner of the saloon.

'And who might you be?' he asked the boy, looking into a face that should have been young but had been aged by illness rather than the passing of years. Greeley guessed that the kid was around twenty, but looked more like fifty when you peered close. It was plain that the crippled arm was the only visible sign of a much more profound ailment.

'I'm Bob Marlin,' the boy said, shocked that anyone in Oaksworth would need to enquire his name. The kid plainly considered himself to be something of a local celebrity.

'Well, Mr Marlin,' Greeley began, a twinkle in his eye but hunger gnawing at his gut, 'who is the fighting man around here?'

Marlin shook his head as if agreeing with himself that this was a difficult question. His face was so narrow that it seemed both of his eye teeth had compensated for a lack of space by crossing inwards over his front teeth.

'The Texans off the trail all carry guns, but we ain't got ourselves no marshal nor no sheriff yet.'

'I wasn't talking guns, Bob,' Greeley laid a hand on the boy's thin shoulder. 'I meant is there anyone in town fancies himself as a pugilist?'

'A what?' the youngster asked, at a loss.

'A man who likes to fight with his fists.'

Bob Marlin understood now, and he smiled. Sideways, his stance and a long, bending neck put Greeley in mind of a vulture. But the boy was friendly and likeable, and now he was coming out with the information Greeley sought.

'Fists or feet, that's Cherokee Dave, mister,' Bob grinned, pleased to have knowledge that this big stranger wanted to share.

'And where will I find Cherokee Dave, Bob?'

'He drinks at Brogan's,' Marlin replied, proud to have been called by his first name, and following close behind Greeley when he started up Main Street.

Brogan's was a false-front building like the rest. Also like the others it had been painted and sign-written, but this was already greying in the weather. With it still being early evening, the place was only about a third full when Greeley walked in the narrow door and stood for a moment to take a look around. There were two bartenders, while a black-haired shapely, lovely but overpainted woman stood behind the bar at the far end.

She was smoking a cigarette and looking boredly around her.

'That's Pat Brogan,' Bob Marlin, the mine of information, said from close behind Greeley, surprising him, not by speaking but through pointing out that Pat Brogan was a woman. Greeley hadn't expected anything but a man to be the proprietor of a rough place like this.

Making up his mind what to do, Greeley took off his coat, tossing it behind him for Marlin to catch. Then he vaulted lightly over the bar. Testing a huge barrel to find that it was full and heavy, he tossed it easily to the top of the counter, ignoring a bartender who was shouting at him.

Vaulting back over the bar, aware that Pat Brogan was advancing slowly, uncertainty showing on her high-cheekboned face, he lifted the barrel above his head with both hands, hearing a gasp of admiration from the boy behind him, and confident that he now had the attention of everyone in the saloon.

Gripping a rim of the wooden keg with the fingers of his right hand, he held it aloft by using just that hand, and he was rewarded by gasps from others awed by his great strength. Mustering all of his strength, wondering if he might be going too far and would ruin the show, he kept the barrel aloft and tossed it to his left hand.

Keeping it going, juggling the heavy barrel from hand to hand above his head, he shouted a challenge. 'Who was the best man here before I arrived?'

'And who might you be, pardner?' a toothless old man called.

'I'm New York Joe,' Greeley replied, using the name from his brief sojourn among the hoboes, stopping the juggling, holding the barrel up with both hands as he added, The heavyweight pugilistic champion of America.'

'And I'm Crazy Horse,' a tall, long-haired cowboy

laughed mockingly.

'Quiet, Hanson,' an elderly, stockily built cattleman silenced what was apparently one of his hands, taking a step forwards to address Greeley. 'I don't know if you're who you say you are, lad, but this here town is sure lacking in sport. Just who would you be prepared to fight?'

'I'll take on all comers,' Greeley promised, placing the barrel back on to the bar top.

The cattleman smiled, and turned to look behind him as several other men sniggered in some kind of expectancy. The rancher beckoned, and the one whom Greeley knew must be Cherokee Dave pushed his way through the crowd to stand facing him.

Dressed in a blue shirt and ordinary Levis, as dark as an Indian, although Greeley took him for a half-breed, the man stood something like six and a half feet. His long black hair fell to a pair of shoulders that resembled those of an ox, while the chest was was deep as the barrel that Greeley had been hefting around.

'This here's Cherokee Dave,' the cattleman said, 'and most folks here in town will put money on him making short work of someone like you, stranger.'

'Then start placing your bets,' Greeley said, half expecting Uncle Elvir to take over the talking, and suddenly saddened when this didn't happen.

The rancher had been right, the town was eager for sport. Within minutes Greeley, with Bob Marlin holding the tail of his jacket so as not to be separated from him, was being pushed along by a seeming multitude that was also moving Cherokee Dave in the same direction. They reached a vacant stock pen beside which Richmond Coles was still organizing the unloading of his saloon. As the crowd formed up around Cherokee Dave and himself, leaving an arena for the contest, Greeley saw Coles walk across to lean on one of the fences that were beginning to support

Aim Before You Draw

rows and rows of spectators. Pat Brogan had come along with the men. Obviously a woman to command respect, she had been placed upon an empty hay wagon to ensure that she had a good view.

Forgetting that he had to do more than just fight now that he was on his own, a sudden realization of this made him call the rancher, who was arguing about a bet, a roll of banknotes in his hand, over to him.

'What's the matter, son?' the cattleman asked, worry creasing his face. 'You ain't about to back out, are ye?'

'I look for fights, not run from them,' Greeley told him, a trace of anger in his voice. 'I want you to know that I ain't going to walk away from this empty handed.'

'You put up a good show, son, and we'll show our appreciation. You have the word of Bill Bradford on that.'

There was general uproar in the crowd as bets were offered and taken. Nobody seemed to be laying much out on Greeley, but that didn't concern him. What was worrying was the faintness from hunger that he was once more beginning to suffer from. It was worsening by the minute.

'Get the show moving, Bradford,' he urged.

'Never seen such a sassy young feller so keen to be slaughtered,' the cattleman chuckled, but he did as Greeley had asked.

The last bets were wagered, and Cherokee Dave was coming confidently forwards. Greeley drove three left hands in quick succession into the face of the half-breed. The punches landed solidly, jarring up through his arm, the knuckles splitting skin, cutting flesh by spreading it tightly over the prominent bones that made Cherokee Dave's rugged face look like it had been carved out of wood.

Greeley had believed his last opponent, Ketchtom, to be tough, but this huge man was walking through his hardest punches as if they were no more than raindrops.

As the half-breed moved in close, Greeley slammed a barrage of punches into his thick body, but they had no effect and the local man wrapped both arms around him in a rib-threatening bear hug. Having seen this coming, and aware that his massive opponent was capable of squeezing the life out of him, Greeley, unable to avoid the aggressive embrace, had kept his arms high and free. Now, as Cherokee Dave gave a little grunt and began to apply pressure, Greeley kneed him hard in the groin while at the same time bringing down both elbows together hard on top of the half-breed's greasy-haired head.

Head and neck driven down into his shoulders, agonized by the knee that had rammed into him, Cherokee Dave released Greeley and stood shaking his head like a bewildered and angry grizzly. Stepping round the big body, Greeley circled it with his left arm to give him leverage as he drove his right fist hard into his opponent's right kidney. Swiftly changing arms, Greeley delivered a vicious punch to the big man's left kidney. There were no rules here other than the natural ones of survival.

Previously unmoved by the blows delivered to his head and body, Cherokee Dave was affected by the kidney punches. Mindful only of the pain wracking his body, he put both hands behind his back in a vain attempt at massaging the agony away.

Presented with a massive stationary target, Greeley went to work, Slamming a combination of hooking and straight-delivered punches to the body, he saw that the new pain he was delivering was adding to what must have been severely damaged kidneys, and the cumulative effect was causing the half-breed to sway. His feet stayed firmly planted but his body did a circular motion as he made no effort to defend himself, despite the crowd, who had a lot of money invested in him, hoarsely shouting encouragement and advice.

Shifting his attack to the head, Greeley smashed Cherokee Dave's nose, ruined his mouth, and belted both eyes until they ballooned to a size that didn't even leave the half-breed with slits to peer through.

The crowd had fallen silent in disbelief at their hero being thrashed so soundly. There was some groaning despair from those who would lose small fortunes if Cherokee Dave didn't recover to make a fight of it. The half-breed was past being able to defend himself, but still he stood as solid as a tree while Greeley pounded his face with his fists.

Knowing that he could never finish this way, Greeley again stepped to the side of and slightly behind his opponent. When he sent in two power-packed punches, left and right, to the kidneys, Cherokee Dave threw back his head and screamed out his agony. It was the harrowing sound of an animal being clumsily slaughtered, but Greeley steeled himself against feeling sympathy. He had once held his punches in New York because an opponent's face had been split grotesquely open, and that opponent had taken advantage, downing Greeley and all but winning the fight. Since then Liam Greeley had neither given nor asked for mercy.

Still behind the half-breed now, he aimed a right hand at the thick back of the big man's neck. His knuckles connected solidly. Toppling forward slowly like a felled tree, Cherokee Dave then hit the dirt with an earthshaking thud that sent clouds of dust up over the spectators.

It was as silent as a grave then. Even the animals in the nearby pens seem to be affected in some supernatural way by the defeat of the local giant. Greeley stood, drawing in deep breaths the way Uncle Elvir had taught him, taking the air deep into his lungs while tensing the muscles of his stomach. Lying at his feet, Cherokee Dave was as still as a corpse. Everything seemed to be held in an invisible cocoon of inaction. Each passing moment seemed to add to the eeriness of the situation.

Then, somewhere distant from the scene, a steer lowed trumpetingly. The sound broke the spell. Somebody cheered, others joined in, then there was applause before the crowd around the impromptu ring surged inwards to praise and congratulate Liam Greeley. Financial losses were ignored, gains forgotten in a concerted admiration for a true fighting man. As Greeley was clapped on the back and shoulders, and hugged by delighted sportsmen, Bob Marlin insistently thrust a hat into his hands. A lanky Texan drawled congratulations to Greeley and tossed a handful of coins into the hat. More coins, and then banknotes followed. Greeley didn't need to go round the crowd with the hat; the people came to him. It overflowed, and Bob Marlin creamed the top off, stuffing notes and coins into his pockets so as to make room for more in the hat. In doing so he explained, unnecessarily, to Greeley that he was merely holding the money for him.

The night had closed in tightly now, and for the first time Greeley realized that his fight with Cherokee Dave had been illuminated in part by flaming torches that some of the men had brought up and attached to the rails of the pens.

With the excitement of the moment over, the crowd was fast dispersing now, people going off to continue interrupted business or seek pleasures different from watching prizefighters. Greeley, the faithful Bob Marlin at his side, walked to where Bill Bradford and two cowboys squatted beside Cherokee Dave, rolling him on to his back and lifting his upper body so that he was in a sitting position.

Standing looking down at the battered half-breed, Greeley suddenly knelt and tipped the contents of the hat on to the ground. He motioned for Bob Marlin to add the money he had in his pockets to the pile. Using the edge of his hand like a butcher's cleaver, only with no force, Greeley parted the heap of money into rough halves. He pushed one half towards Bradford.

'See that he gets that, will you please?'

Bradford nodded. 'I'll fix him up, don't worry.' He looked up at Greeley. 'You're a decent fellow. What did you say your name is, Joe?'

'It's Liam Greeley, and I am the American heavyweight champion.'

'No one in this district will ever doubt that now,' Bill Bradford called after Greeley as he walked away with the scrammed-armed Bob Marlin at his side.

Going straight to Belber's general store, Greeley bought himself new pants, shirt, vest and jacket. Changing out back, he tossed the clothes that had been ripped and dirtied by riding the rods, including the homesteader's shirt, into the trash can.

'You look like a million dollars,' Bob Marlin, his eyes popping, exclaimed as Greeley walked back into the main part of the store.

Although he wouldn't have admitted it to the kid, Greeley felt like a million dollars. His instant wealth on coming to Oaksworth confirmed his original feeling that this was his town. Paying for his clothes, Greeley purchased a new hat for an overly grateful Bob Marlin.

'Where to now, Mr Greeley?' the boy asked when they were standing out where a sidewalk would be when Oaksworth came of age.

About to say 'I', Greeley changed it to 'we'. It wouldn't hurt to have the kid tag along with him. He could be a good luck charm. Even if not, Greeley had come to like the intense young Bob Marlin, so he said, 'We'll go to the barber shop, Bob, and get me a shave. Then I'm going to eat myself the biggest meal you can get in this town, before I book myself a bed for the night.'

As Greeley relaxed in a chair being shaved, Bob

Marlin walked impatiently up and down the shop. In his earnest way of speaking he fixed Greeley up with his next two needs: food and a bed. Bob's sister, Elizabeth, rented the rear section of the Cattleman's Cottage saloon and gambling joint, which was owned by brothers Jim and Denis Moore.

'Couldn't do better than that,' the barber put in without being asked. 'The Moore brothers are real gentlemen, and the "cottage" is the most respectable place in Oaksworth.'

Gratified by the recommendation, but irritated by the interruption, Bob Marlin rushed out more words. 'Elizabeth runs an eating place there . . .'

'Best food in Oaksworth,' the barber interjected, gaining an angry glare from Bob Marlin.

'And we've got some spare rooms,' the boy finished what he wanted to say, 'so Elizabeth will let you stay there.'

But when Marlin introduced Greeley to his demure, plain-featured sweet sister, Elizabeth Marlin seemed to be put off by Greeley's size, the fact that he was a stranger in town, and, above all, his reputation as a man of violence – her brother having given her a garbled but blow-by-blow account of the destruction of Cherokee Dave. In the end it was, Greeley felt certain, a combination of two things that persuaded the girl to give him a room. First it was her brother's whining, persistent persuading, and second that she obviously needed the money.

Yet he found that her restaurant was very popular with the business people of the town. Elizabeth waited on the tables, and employed a Mexican woman to do the cooking. She seated Greeley alone at a small table, upsetting her brother by adamantly refusing to allow him to join his hero at the table. The meal was large and excellently cooked. As he ate, Greeley, the hard times, the starving times on the road running through his mind, savoured and was grateful for every morsel.

All the time he ate he was conscious of two men at a nearby table covertly watching him. They were middle-aged, elegantly dressed men with the high collared shirts favoured by bankers. As Greeley laid down his knife and fork and took a mouthful of coffee, the one who appeared to be the elder of the two men stood and walked hesitantly over to his table. He was below average height, slightly stooped, and with a pot belly. From a short distance his complexion looked to be purple, but as he neared Greeley could see this was an illusion created by a myriad of broken veins under the skin of his face. Sandy-coloured hair ringed a bald pate, and the small bristling moustache was darker, being tinged with red.

'Please forgive this intrusion. I am James Moore,' the man said, doing a quarter turn to stretch an indicating arm to where his companion still sat at their table. 'This is my brother, Denis.'

Denis Moore raised a hand in half-greeting, as yet unsure how his brother's approach would be treated. A year or two younger, he differed from James only by being bespectacled and having slightly more hair.

Standing, extending his right hand, Greeley started to say, 'I'm . . .'

'Your fame has travelled ahead of you, Mr Greeley,' James Moore said with a businessman's practised smile that put small, yellowing teeth on show, shaking Greeley by the hand.

'What can I do for you, Mr Moore?' Greeley asked, and the other man looked rueful as he absently ran a hand through what remained of his hair.

'I'm not normally indecisive, Mr Greeley, believe me, but right now I can't give a definitive answer to your question. Intuition urged me, and my brother, I should add, to make your acquaintance. I wonder if you would care to take your coffee at our table.'

Elizabeth Marlin, with rows of cups and a supply of coffee on a table placed just outside of the kitchen, brought coffee to the bigger table as Greeley joined the Moore brothers. They both stayed silent until Elizabeth, who had a similar kind of modest appeal to that of her crippled brother, had left the table.

Looking round at the other diners, refined men with dignified wives, both seemingly out of place in a turbulent town such as Oaksworth, James Moore commented, 'We need to encourage more enterprising people such as Miss Marlin. Respectable people with well-run businesses provide the kind of foundation that we must construct Oaksworth on.'

'We don't approve of violence, Mr Greeley,' Denis Moore spoke for the first time, and Greeley was soon to discover that the two brothers carried on conversation as a kind of double act.

'We did, of course, hear of the incident involving that rather unfortunate local man,' James said with a dismissive shrug, 'and while we can't possibly condone such behaviour . . .'

'We respect your right to follow your profession,' Denis put in, 'just as we provide gambling facilities, strictly regulated and scrupulously fair, because that is what a cow town demands.'

Nodding in agreement with his brother, James Moore told Greeley, 'Bill Bradford spoke most highly of you. A solid man that, Mr Greeley, someone we welcome as a new citizen of Oaksworth.'

'I was under the impression Bradford is a cattle-driver,' Greeley spoke for the first time since sitting at the table.

'*Was* a drover,' Denis laid emphasis on the past tense. 'Mr Bradford is the proprietor of a large ranch in Texas, good sir. He is forsaking the trail, delegating that side of his business to a foreman, while he establishes himself here as a cattle agent.'

'We are on the threshold of great things here in Oaksworth, Mr Greeley.' James Moore was buzzing with excitement. 'What you see out there now is nothing compared to what will be. Within a short time cattle-drivers will discover that Abilene is a closed market. That is why Oaksworth must be built up most carefully. To this end we are in the process of forming a town council. At present it consists of Merton Raines, the barber, Thomas Bent, the general merchant, Bill Bradford, and Denis and myself.'

'Naturally, with the town in a state of flux, elections are out of the question. At this stage we are simply co-opting members,' Denis said.

This talk of forming a council had Greeley hoping that his first day in Oaksworth, very rewarding up to then, was going to take yet another upward turn by his being co-opted on to the local council. In at the beginning, he knew that he had what it took to get to the top, right to the top.

'Why are you telling me this?' he asked to have one or both brothers come to their point.

It was James who replied, disappointing him. 'You are a powerful man, Mr Greeley, a man whose presence will have a subduing, a stabilizing effect on the rougher element coming to this town.'

All wasn't lost. A position as councillor wasn't on offer, yet, but it looked as if they were going to ask him to be the law in Oaksworth.

'The thing is, Mr Greeley,' James Moore was going on to deliver the final blow to Greeley's hopes, 'we would like to offer you a position within our organization.'

'What sort of position?' asked Greeley dejectedly.

Spreading his hands wide, palms up, James Moore said, 'It's wide open. Dealer, bartender, a sort of regulator? Call on us tomorrow and take a look around, Mr Greeley. The choice is yours.'

Getting the message, that the Moores were prepared to give him any job providing he was there to take care of trouble as it arose, Greeley didn't like their double standards where violence was concerned. Yet he didn't turn them down out of hand. Tomorrow he would probe all the possibilities that Oaksworth presented. There was no immediate rush, for the money thrown in the hat after the fight would support him for some time. It occurred to him that he might need to take up the offer made by the Moore brothers while he awaited another, better prospect.

'We don't, of course, expect an immediate answer,' James Moore said.

'I will come to see you tomorrow,' Greeley promised as he rose from the table. 'Now, if you will excuse me, gentlemen.'

Bob Marlin waited outside for him like a well-trained dog, although he fell in at Greeley's side rather than to heel. As he headed for Pat Brogan's place, Greeley asked. 'Does your sister permit you to drink, Bob?'

'No, but I can go in with you,' the crippled boy replied, thankful for being able to walk into a saloon with the man the whole town admired.

This time the place was packed. Those nearest to Greeley recognized him, but he could identify no one other than the owner, who stood in her usual place at the end of the bar. Neither Cherokee Dave nor Bill Bradford were there. Cowboys danced wildly, spurs jangling, long legs going dangerously this way and that. Their partners were girls whose faces were painted even in excess of Pat Brogan's brightly coloured features.

At the bar Greeley ordered a rye. When it came, the bartender, made prominent by his effeminacy among so many rough men, said mincingly. 'It's on the house.'

When Greeley looked down the bar at Pat Brogan, she raised her glass to him and smiled. He walked to her, noticing that Bob Marlin's licence granted by his sister didn't extend to mixing with painted women. The boy stood waiting, hurt in his eyes as Greeley walked away.

'My,' Pat Brogan greeted him, and he was pained to notice how the unnecessary cosmetics marred her natural beauty, 'you look real smart. What happened to the bum I first saw?'

'Some of us are capable of changing ourselves,' he replied, too harshly to someone who had just bought him a drink.

Maybe he caused her to blink, but she soon recovered. 'I take it, Greeley, that you have no objection to a Calico Queen buying you a drink.'

His name had become known, he realized. Pat Brogan wasn't putting herself down by referring to herself as a 'Calico Queen'. Up close, though she still had a just-below-the-surface loveliness, life had case-hardened her in a way that made her profession evident.

'None at all . . .' he started to assure her, but a disturbance some little way from them took her attention. Touching his arm in a gesture that said she would come back to him, Pat Brogan walked away.

Liam Greeley decided not to wait. Now enjoying money and food again there remained only one more thing of which he had been deprived, which was sleep. Walking over to collect Bob Marlin in a way that had become quickly automatic to him, Greeley was going out of the door as Richmond Coles came in.

Darkly handsome, poised and superbly dressed, Coles was closely followed by a wiry man who wore two guns in holsters attached to crossed belts, and was all the time alert, ceaselessly watching for any possible threat to Coles, eyes constantly flicking from left to right and back again. Coles blocked Greeley's exit, a friendly smile lighting up the dark-skinned face.

'Well, well, it's the fighting man,' Coles said, not mockingly but in recognition. 'I wonder if you would do me the favour of joining me in a convivial drink?'

Greeley was undecided. He wanted to once again sample the comfort of a bed, but before that he intended to write to Martha Jane to tell her where he had settled, and repeat in pen his verbal promise to send for her.

'I have a proposition that will be of immense mutual benefit,' Richmond Coles told him.

Shrugging, telling himself that Oaksworth had done him proud up to then, and that he had nothing to lose by delaying bed a short while, Greeley turned and walked back into Brogan's with Richmond Coles.

FOUR

It was the morning of the day when the American Playground was to open. The three of them, Liam Greeley, Richmond Coles, and Rafe Kennedy, the two-gun man who watched over Coles day and night, stood in the wasteland at the rear of the building. James and Denis Moore had offered Greeley an undefined job, respectability, and, perhaps, eventual status in the town. Coles had offered employment as troubleshooter in his saloon, adventure, and a chance to get ahead rapidly. Against the outspoken advice of Bob Marlin, and the silent disapproval of his sister, Greeley had taken up the latter offer. Right now Coles, who knew what Greeley could do with his fists, was anxious for Kennedy to begin teaching him gun-slinging. Having given Greeley a gunbelt, holster, and Colt .45, Richmond Coles spoke to Greeley as Kennedy lined up seven bottles along the edge of an upturned, rotting haulier's cart.

'All we'll concentrate on this morning, Liam, is having Rafe show you how to aim and shoot. Take it slowly. There'll be plenty of time to learn a fast draw when you're able to hit what you're pointing your six-shooter at,' Richmond Coles said.

Kennedy was walking back towards them, his hawkish face serious as he drew one of his guns and got ready to give Greeley a demonstration.

'I'd like to try a draw,' Greeley said, his words causing a rare smile to flit across Kennedy's normally sullen features.

'Don't try to run before you can walk, Liam,' Coles advised, turning to Kennedy. 'Show him how to hold a gun properly, Rafe.'

The remembered, monotonous drone of Uncle Elvir's voice giving instructions, over and over again, ran through Greeley's mind, and his fingers itched as he recalled the endless succession of days on which he had practised for hour after hour.

'Surely drawing the gun isn't all that difficult,' he queried.

'It takes years to learn,' an exasperated Richmond Coles said, 'and then few people ever perfect it.'

'I thought it just went like this,' Greeley said in a deceptively conversational way.

Then he drew and fired. His movement was a blur, the six shots he fired close enough together to sound as one, six of the bottles seeming to shatter in one single explosion. As his two companions stood dumbfounded, Greeley spun the trigger guard of his .45 on a finger, plucked a bullet from his belt, reloading one chamber and dropping the gun back in its holster in one smooth flourish.

As Coles was about to say something but was too taken aback to get a word out, Greeley drew again and fired. Although the final bottle exploded into fragments, Greeley had reholstered his gun before the other two had realized what had happened.

Calmly taking his .45 out again and leisurely reloading it, he asked Coles, 'You were saying, Richmond?'

'You worry me, Greeley,' Coles said seriously, his face having paled.

'Why?' Greeley enquired, spinning his gun forwards, backwards, then forwards and back into its holster in mid spin. 'You want someone to take care of your place, and now you know that I can do it.'

'That's fair enough,' Coles acknowledged with a solemn nod of his head. 'But the way I see it, we are both ambitious men, and that could mean trouble.'

'Only if we're both after the same thing, Coles,' Greeley pointed out.

'What is it you're after, Liam?'

'I'm not sure yet,' said Greeley, and a pensive Coles walked slowly away, going slowly back into his saloon. Without a word to Greeley, Kennedy followed his master.

That night Greeley policed the saloon with no problems. Though not a gambling man himself, he was astute enough to know that every game was played well in favour of the house. Most of the cowboys came to know it too, but they didn't want to argue when a big man like Greeley, with an even bigger reputation, was there ready to deal with them.

In the early hours of the morning, when the only remaining customers were drunks and half-drunks that the bartenders could handle, Richmond Coles called Greeley into his office at the back. Gesturing Greeley into an ornate and comfortable seat, Coles poured him a stiff drink before speaking.

'We have a problem,' Coles began carefully, hands together prayer-fashion, fingertips against his lips in thoughtful pose, 'in that we are very much alike. Not physically, for I could never match your strength, your ability as a pugilist, nor your amazing speed with a gun. But we are both here in Oaksworth to amass money and personal esteem; both those things equalling power. At the moment you are my employee, but with your talents you have no need to remain in that position. In every case of emancipation the slave rises above the master, Liam.'

'I understand that,' Greeley said, draining his glass,

holding it out to Coles, who was ready to refill it. 'But you overlook one thing, Richmond. I need you to show me the way.'

'Ah, that is so,' Coles gave a wistful little smile. 'But what of when I have taught you all you need to know?'

Shrugging his wide shoulders, Greeley offered, 'That's something we'll have to leave to chance.'

'Oh no, Liam,' Coles stood, coming out from behind his desk to pace slowly round his opulent office. 'Tonight the house was a winner, and that's how it will be every night, as I never leave anything to chance.'

This admission confirmed for Greeley that the games were rigged. Letting that matter rest, he asked, 'Then how do you see things, Richmond?'

'Most problems are simple, Liam, It's people who complicate them.'

'So there's an easy answer to the problem you see here?' Greeley checked.

'There is. Either you gun me down here and now, and I have no protection because Kennedy is riding to Abilene on a message for me, or I have you shot in the back outside in the shadows one night.'

'That way one of us has to lose,' Greeley remarked. 'If this is as simple as you claim, isn't there some way we can both win?'

Propping himself on the edge of his desk, Coles looked keenly at Greeley. 'There is, Liam. You are an intelligent man, but you lack my cunning. I am, I believe, just as intelligent, but I can't fight the way you can. With your help, I can own this town while looking after you at all times. My cunning and your skill with fists and a gun, Liam, an unbeatable combination.'

'There's one thing you've missed, Richmond. When you own the town, I could put a bullet in your head and take over.'

'I didn't miss that possibility, Liam. The thing is,

you are capable of killing me and taking over the town, but then you'd find that you lacked the cunning to keep it.'

Laughing, genuinely amused at Coles's inarguable logic, Greeley stood. Out of habit instilled by Uncle Elvir, he was concerned about being very late getting back to his room. In a short time the two Marlins and he had become something like a family.

'So, Richmond,' he said. 'You have figured all the angles, which means that you have me here for some reason.'

'I would suggest a gentleman's agreement, Liam,' Coles replied.

'Can we trust each other?' Greeley queried.

'I don't know,' Coles replied gravely, but then he extended his right hand, 'but for the first time in my life I have no option but to take a chance.'

Taking the hand, shaking it, Greeley said, 'You can rely on me. I never go back on my word.'

'And you can trust me.'

'If I find that I can't, then I can kill you,' Greeley said quietly, going out of the door, leaving Richmond Coles in no doubt that he meant what he said.

Out in the dark and deserted dirt street, Greeley accepted that he needed Coles. Although far from being a slow thinker, Greeley was rusty in the scheming department of his brain from lack of use. Uncle Elvir had always taken care of the planning, and until Greeley had perfected the finer points he would rely on Coles. Maybe the time would come when the handshake he had just shared with the saloon owner would become invalid. If that should happen, then Greeley would deal with it however the prevailing circumstances demanded. In the meantime, unless Coles tried to rig the game they were playing together as he did the blackjack, faro and the like in his saloon, Greeley was happy with things the way they were.

As he walked in the direction of his new home in the rear section of of the Cattleman's Cottage, so did he gradually, with a great deal of effort, form in his mind the letter that he intended to write to Martha Jane before he turned in. Not having been in Oaksworth long enough to have become a target, he kept to the centre of Main Street, his mind fully concentrated on the projected letter.

Despite his inattention, instinct took over as a shot was fired and a bullet passed so close to his head that the hissing whistle it made went on in his ear after it had passed. Leaping to his right, Greeley sought the concealing shadow cast by a building, and his shoulder slammed against the front well of the butcher's shop. Drawing his .45 he waited, wondering. It didn't seem likely that his agreement with Coles had expired so swiftly. But he couldn't think of anyone who would be his enemy after so short a time in town.

He heard a sound then. At first he didn't trust his ears for it was a low chortle of amusement. Greeley judged that it came from outside of the Smoky River Bank, one of the few buildings in Oaksworth able to boast a boardwalk running along its length. The sound came again, and it definitely was guarded laughter. Then a voice called to him in a husky whisper.

'Watch yourself, mister. Some trailhand bet Pat Brogan fifty dollars that she wouldn't walk down Main Street unclothed. She's doing it right now, mister, only with a six-shooter in each hand to blast the head off any man who takes a peek at her.'

Just as the man across the street finished speaking, a shot rang out and he cursed, leaping off the sidewalk into the street, running away with bullets kicking up the dust around him. Greeley thought the man was hit when he fell face down. But it was a trip, and he was soon up and running to vanish into the night.

'You there, skulking by the butcher's shop, you want

some of the same?' Pat Brogan's voice called shrilly from the dark between two buildings diagonally across the street from Greeley.

'All I'm looking for is to go to my bed,' he called back.

There was a long pause, then the woman asked querulously. 'Is that you over there, Liam Greeley?'

'It is.'

Having identified himself, he strode across the street to where he knew Pat Brogan was standing. As he went he took off his jacket, his stride not faltering as he heard the distinct clicks of two trigger-hammers being drawn back.

'You're just one step from having a hole blown in your head, Greeley,' she warned, but there was a tremor in her voice and he continued to advance on her, although the shadows still hid her from him.

'Have you won your bet?' he asked, able now to see a white blur that was her body.

'I've done what I said I'd do.'

'Then put this on,' he said, averting his face and holding his jacket out at arm's length.

Greeley heard the double metallic clunk that told of him she must have stooped to put both of her six-guns on the ground. A little while later he detected the scraping sound of her picking them up. Then Pat Brogan stepped out in front of him, his jacket huge on her, the shoulders falling down at each side and the rest of it covering her almost to the knees. She was picking her way carefully on bare feet.

Huddling in the jacket, giving a little shiver, she told him 'You'll never know how good it feels to be handed a coat in the night.'

'I've got a rough idea,' he said, and she couldn't see his grin in the dark.

What she had done was the act of a wild woman caught up in new-town craziness. Now that it was over she was suffering the reaction felt by everyone who behaves rashly. After she had tried a few faltering steps on tip-toe to protect the soles of her feet, he picked her up effortlessly in his arms. She felt soft and womanly, and her perfume stirred at him as he carried her up Main Street to her saloon.

Pat Brogan gave him a coy little smile as he set her down on her feet inside of the door. In the subdued half lights of the saloon he saw a drunk sitting on a stool, his arms and head resting on the bar, his snores as rasping as a sawmill working at full blast. The only other person present was one of Pat Brogan's dancing girls. She was tipsy, her dress hanging low off her shoulders. Unaware of their entrance the girl was staggering behind the bar, picking up a full bottle of whiskey. As the girl was raising the bottle to her mouth, Pat strode angrily up to her, a ludicrous figure in the over-large jacket. But this didn't affect her movements. Snatching the bottle away from the girl with her left hand, she backhanded her hard with the right. Greeley saw the impact of the blow knock the girl's head round. When she ran in terror from the bar up the stairs, blood was leaking from her nose and the corners of her mouth.

'Thieving bitch,' Pat Brogan snarled contemptuously, then switched to a smile for Greeley. 'I thank you kindly for bringing me home, sir. Let me pour you a drink.'

The offer was tempting, but Greeley was certain both the Marlins would be lying awake, timing his arrival home. Then there was Martha Jane, to whom he was right then being unfaithful by eyeing Pat Brogan, who looked really cute dressed in his jacket and nothing else.

'Some other time,' he said, forcing himself to be firm.

It wouldn't be wise for him to stay any longer. There would have been eyes out there in the night, furtive eyes avid for a glimpse of Pat winning her bet. Those same eyes would have seen him carry her home, and would be waiting now to see what time he left.

Pouring herself a drink, she looked at him archly. 'It would be fair of me to give you half the fifty dollars that I've won.'

'The money's yours, goodnight,' he said, turning to leave.

'You are a difficult man to repay. There's a bed here for you tonight. At least you won't refuse that.'

'Sorry,' he said, making his way to the door.

'Wait!'

Pat Brogan almost shouted the one word command, causing Greeley automatically to pause and turn. She had climbed to the third stair, facing him. Undoing the buttons of his jacket, she slipped it off, fully revealing her body as she held the garment out to him.

'Take your coat with you.'

A battle raged within him, with sound sense being the victor. Leaving her holding his jacket, he strode resolutely from Pat Brogan's saloon. Yet he took her with him inside of his head. She was pushing out Martha Jane and the letter that he wanted to write.

It was no better when he got back. Stealthily going along a creaking landing, hoping not to disturb either Bob or Elizabeth, he lit the oil lamp when he reached his room. With difficulty, he forced away thoughts of Pat Brogan and wrote a letter with which he was pleased. It was an exercise that brought an image of the lovely, sweet, decent Martha Jane into his head.

But the following day, when he was eating in Elizabeth's restaurant, Pat Brogan was back, filling his mind to such an extent that James Moore had to speak to him twice before Greeley realized that the hotelier/saloon keeper was standing by his table.

'May I sit?'

'Of course,' Greeley answered, gesturing to a chair.

Sitting, Moore waited until Elizabeth had taken his

order and had departed before he spoke again. 'If I may say so, Mr Greeley, you have made an unwise choice.'

'I don't agree,' Greeley replied, aware that Moore was referring to his going to work for Richmond Coles. 'Both the pay and the prospects suit me, Mr Moore.'

'A short-term outlook, if you will forgive me for saying so,' James Moore said, his small eyes studying Greeley intently. 'I admit that the American Playground has a certain gaudy attractiveness that the cowboys seem to like, but compare it for a moment with the Cattleman's Cottage, Mr Greeley. Our hotel side of the business already has sixty rooms, and more will be added as the town grows. We are going places, Mr Greeley, and it was the fervent wish of my brother and myself that you would go with us.'

Greeley shrugged to cover his own uncertainty about the choice he had made. 'As I said, Mr Moore, Coles pays well and he would also seem to be "going places", as you put it.'

'I am afraid that is all too true,' James Moore said regretfully as his brother came to the table and sat without being asked. James spoke to the newcomer. 'You tell Mr Greeley, Denis.'

'This afternoon,' Denis Moore began, taking on a shrunken-eyed appearance as he removed his spectacles to clean them. 'This afternoon, not more than an hour ago, Richmond Coles and five of his associates forced themselves on to the town council.'

'Which means that we original members are outnumbered,' James Moore said in a funereal tone.

Keeping a poker face, Greeley felt himself leaping about excitedly inside. Coles's audacity, and the speed at which he worked, was amazing. Rejoicing at having made an agreement last night with this go-ahead man, Greeley, however, couldn't help but feel more than a tinge of sympathy for the Moore brothers, who were trying to ensure that Oaksworth was brought through its infant days into maturity in a correct and proper way.

'I think you should broach the major issue, Jim,' Denis Moore said, and his brother nodded, clearing his throat noisily.

'This is something that has to be said so that there will be no misunderstanding, Mr Greeley,' James Moore said gravely. 'Once Richmond Coles was established on the council, he moved that a jail should be built and yourself be appointed as town marshal. We, that is my brother, those who set up the council with us originally, and myself, vigorously opposed the proposal. What is more, we shall continue to do so.'

'Not because of any personal animosity towards your good self,' Denis Moore put it.

'Indeed no,' his brother agreed. 'In different circumstances we would be delighted that the good citizens of our town could sleep safely in their beds with you as the law in Oaksworth'

'In different circumstances,' Denis stressed his brother's proviso.

'And what are these "different circumstances?' Greeley asked, with an eerie feeling that he was putting the question for Uncle Elvir.

'You would need to be completely independent of Richmond Coles,' James told him unequivocally.

'Completely independent,' Denis emphasized.

His meal finished, Greeley stood, looking from one to the other of the brothers as he said, 'As I have already accepted employment with Richmond Coles, I could never be entirely independent of him again. Now, if you will excuse me, gentlemen.'

'You do appreciate that there is nothing personal in this, Mr Greeley,' James Moore said pleadingly.

'Nothing personal at all,' his brother added.

'I fully understand your position, gentlemen,' Greeley assured them. As he was about to leave the restaurant the sound of two rapid gunshots in succession came from the main part of the building.

Instant apprehension froze occupants of the restaurant into immobility. Both of the Moore brothers had stood up in shock, but made no other move. Elizabeth Marlin stood with a coffee jug poised above a cup, and the other diners flicked their eyes fearfully from side to side, convinced that they were in danger and trying to anticipate the direction from which it would come.

Then the spell was broken as an agitated Bob Marlin, his useless arm held higher than usual, burst into the restaurant, gabbling out words to the Moore brothers. 'Mr Moore, Mr Moore,' the boy addressed them separately. 'There's a man shooting up the saloon.'

'Nobody hurt?' James Moore tried to make it a statement rather than a question, wanting it to be so.

'He shot Ken Glover's thumb right off,' the crippled boy related the fate of one bartender.

'Is he a tall man, kid? Moustache and a short little beard? All kinda dressed up in black and white clothes?'

All eyes turned to a table in a corner where the man who had asked the questions sat. In his thirties, his fastidious way of dressing had him look more like a lawyer than a trail-rider. Most striking was the long hair that fell below his shoulders. The colour of it went beyond a description of fair. The hair was a brilliant white.

'That's Marion Clay, a Tennessean,' the stranger said to no one in particular. 'I thought I saw him riding in.'

'A drunk,' James Moore exclaimed.

'Clay's no drunk, he's just mean,' the white-haired man said.

The report of another shot echoed in the restaurant, and James Moore, pale of face, said to his brother, 'Come, Denis, we'll have to put a stop to this.'

'Stay where you are,' the stranger advised, eating his

meal, the only one in the restaurant to be carrying on normally. 'So far as I know Clay's credited with twenty-one killings. It won't worry him none to add you two to his tally.'

Looking steadily at the white-haired man, who was still eating, totally unmoved, Greeley said, 'You seem to know a lot about this Marion Clay, mister.'

'Well,' the stranger began, pausing to put a forkful of food into his mouth to chew contentedly on it, 'I guess I know enough to stay in here while he's out there.'

There had been no sign of fear, no cowardice in the way the man said this. It was a simple case of him making what he saw as a true statement.

'Stay here, both of you,' Greeley told the Moore brothers.

Going out of the restaurant, not the direct way through to the saloon, but out of a side door, he walked round to the front of the building. A jet black horse was at the hitching-rail outside the saloon as Greeley headed for the door. Hearing footsteps close behind him, not having to turn to see who it was, Greeley ordered, 'You keep right back out of it, Bob.'

He went into a saloon, where a man wearing the contrasting blacks and whites mentioned by the white-haired man in the restaurant leaned with his elbows on the bar, toying with a glass of whiskey from which it was obvious he hadn't taken one sip. There were two bartenders present, one whose hands trembled visibly as he made a pretence of wiping glasses. The second was clutching a hand wrapped in a bloody bar towel, and looked in danger of passing out.

As Greeley walked up to stand a few feet from him, the man in black and white turned his head slightly, speaking as if answering a question, although Greeley hadn't uttered a word. 'Yes, I fought on the Confederate side in the war.'

His glossy black hair was wavy and well-groomed.

The eyes that coolly surveyed Greeley were dark blue, and the short beard and moustache the white-haired man had described were neatly trimmed. Turning his head away from Greeley, he raised his glass as if he was about to drink. But it didn't reach his lips. He placed the glass on the bar top, his movements as quick and sure as a cat.

'Marion Clay?' Greeley asked.

'From Washita,' Clay nodded confirmation of his name, still facing forward.

'What are you doing here in Oaksworth?'

'You the law around here?'

'No.'

Doing a quarter turn towards Greeley, resting his left elbow easily on the bar, Clay said with a mirthless smile. 'Then I could say that what I'm doing here is my business. But you look like a nice enough gent, so I'll tell you. I'm here to smoke up this town and to drill anybody who tries to stop me. Now, who are you?'

'I'm the man who's going to stop you,' Greeley informed him quietly.

The beard moved as a smile brightened Clay's face. Then the smile was gone, and he nodded what seemed to be pleased assent to what Greeley had said. Turning to face his front once more, Marion Clay said in a friendly way, 'This is something that I'll be happy to discuss with you, but please permit me to finish my drink first.'

Greeley watched, every muscle, every nerve in his body not tense but in a relaxed kind of state that was for him preparation for action, as Clay lifted his glass with his right hand.

Having already decided that the whiskey was no more than an excuse for Clay to be in the saloon, and that the man didn't touch alcohol, Greeley knew that the glass would once again not touch the beard and moustached-rimmed lips.

He was right. Clay tilted his head back a little and parted his lips in pretence. Then he dropped the glass and his gun came out of his holster to fill his hand as if by magic. Staying cool, thinking with amusement that Marion Clay was a man Uncle Elvir would have been proud to have trained, Greeley aimed before he drew, and drew so fast that his bullet had split Marion Clay's heart asunder before he could accurately level his gun. Clay did fire, but it was a post-death reflex action that sent a bullet harmlessly into the floor.

People were crammed in the doorway now, among them the two Moore brothers. The white-haired man came through them to walk over and look down dispassionately at the dead body lying crookedly against the bar, to say wonderingly, 'I didn't think there were two men faster than Marion Clay!'

'Who is the other man?' Greeley asked.

But the white-haired man, well-built but no more than of average height, didn't reply. Walking slowly to the door the crowd parted to let him out.

FIVE

Shortly after he had gunned down Marion Clay, Liam Greeley was appointed town marshal in Oaksworth. With the Moore brothers beholden to him for saving their property and probably their lives, neither they nor their more conservative colleagues on the council could oppose the motion. A solid jail was constructed without delay, and Greeley after promising Elizabeth that her brother would come to no harm, had taken on the crippled Bob Marlin as jailer at the so far unoccupied town prison and marshal's office combined.

In the few weeks that had passed since then the town had grown beyond all expectations. The 50,000 Longhorns that had been in the pens when Greeley had arrived had now been joined by a further 100,000, all of them awaiting a rise in prices. Two more large gambling hells had sprung up on Main Street, Jud Parkins's Grand Slam and Hugh Hartman's Golden Wheel. Those crowding into Oaksworth to seek fun and fortunes discovered that these two places had all the inviting gaudiness of Richmond Coles's American Playground, but their games were a little less biased in favour of the house than were those in Coles's place. The wiser majority, however, soon discovered that the much more refined and sophisticated Cattleman's Cottage was run fairly and offered the only dependable gambling in town. As a result, both of the new businesses suffered to a modest extent, but the American Playground was badly hit. Trade fell to an unprofitable low.

All of this led up to the evening when Greeley, who still lived with the Marlins, had to reluctantly carry out a task that was certain to provoke anger and acrimony, but would redress the balance of Oaksworth's gambling business in favour of the American Playground and its owner Richmond Coles. As marshal he was paid $150 a month by the town, plus two dollars per conviction for those persons he arrested, yet overriding this was his liaison with Richmond Coles.

So it was that with a heavy heart he bid goodnight to Elizabeth and Bob, to begin his nightly rounds at the Moore brothers' premises. Outside of the door, in a strategic position, Greeley posted a broadside reading: ALL FIREARMS MUST BE DEPOSITED WITH THE PROPRIETORS. There were muttered complaints from disgruntled cowboys who paused to read the notice over his shoulder.

Going inside then, Greeley was surprised to see the white-haired man sitting alone, back against the wall. Since the Clay shooting he had caught a glimpse of the man just once, apparently making a small purchase at the general store. With this man of mystery back in town, Greeley made a mental note to keep an eye on him as he went to a wall and affixed another of his broadsides. Greeley had posted two more, amid angry comments and remarks, when James Moore came hurrying up to him, eyes swinging between the poster nearest to Greeley.

'What's all this?' he demanded, more bemused than he was angry.

'New rules, tell your bartenders to take everyone's gun when they enter and not return them until they leave.'

'Where did this rule come from?' James Moore asked snappily.

'Yes, whose rule is it?' Denis Moore came up to support his brother.

'Mine, as town marshal.'

'I'm not sure that a marshal has the power to impose such a rule,' James complained.

'I certainly wouldn't have thought so,' Denis seconded the contention.

'Bring it up at the next council meeting,' Greeley suggested helpfully. The brothers wouldn't get far against him with the council, and he found that he was enjoying himself. The task he had dreaded as a necessary chore was giving him a good feeling. Drawing his revolver he rapped the butt on the bar for silence. First the tinkling of a piano died away, then voices raised raucously quietened, then the buzz of normal coversation faded to leave a silence in which every eye was on him.

'All of you have by now had time to read these broadsides. They mean exactly what they say. I will be back here in one hour. Anyone still carrying a gun then will be locked up.'

Before he could reach the door and go out, James Moore was beside him, asking, 'Is the same rule being enforced at all the other houses on Main Street?'

'The American Playground, for instance?' Denis Moore pointedly asked.

A little ashamed of himself, Liam Greeley walked away from them without giving an answer and stepped out into the crowded street. As he walked tall along Main Street, the silver badge glistening on his chest, both townsfolk and strangers moved aside to provide a clear path for him. It didn't peak as did the adulation he had received as a pugilist in New York, but this had a different, constant throb of respect that he found to be equally intoxicating, perhaps even more so.

Approaching Coles's place, Greeley felt a little uncomfortable at the thought of having none of the broadsides he had posted at the Cattleman's Cottage. He actually winced when he saw the huge banner draped across the front of the premises. In tall and garish red letters it proclaimed EVERYTHING GOES AT THE AMERICAN PLAYGROUND. It was a clear message to the citizens of Oaksworth, the Moore brothers in particular, that the law stopped at the door of Richmond Coles's gambling palace.

Finding Coles standing as an observer by one of the gaming tables, Greeley said in a low tone, 'I'd have preferred it for you to have been a little more subtle, Richmond.'

'Subtlety is for the faint-hearted in both love and war, Liam,' Coles said with a smile. 'We must be daring to achieve our aims. Now, hadn't you better return to the Cattleman's Cottage and enforce the law?'

Finding that he was eager to get away from the man who could loosely be referred to as his 'partner', Greeley was halfway across the floor when Coles caught up with him, placing a friendly hand on his shoulder. 'Incidentally, Liam, your work load will be eased as from tomorrow morning, when you gain a deputy.'

'I don't need a deputy,' Greeley objected vehemently. 'I can handle anything that crops up in Oaksworth.'

'At present, I agree, Liam. But soon you will be moving on to bigger things.'

'What bigger things?' Greeley asked, a part of him apprehensive about what Coles was arranging, the major part of him eager for advancement, whatever it might be.

Stopping him with a raised hand and a little chuckle at his ardent question, Coles said. 'All in good time, Liam, all in good time.'

Accepting that he would learn nothing more from

Coles on that issue at the moment, Greeley was moving away but paused to enquire, 'Who will my deputy be?'

'Rafe Kennedy, Liam, Rafe Kennedy.'

Greeley found that the name gave him a brief feeling of chill. He knew little or nothing of Kennedy, but the taciturn two-gun-man struck him as a bad lot. Honest enough with himself to admit that he was allowing his ambition to blur, perhaps even twist his line of honesty, Greeley saw a massive difference between that and a person of Kennedy's character becoming an officer of the law.

Turning this over in his mind, he made his way back down to the Cattleman's Cottage. Relying on his reputation with fists and guns to have done the job for him in advance, his only reservation when he reached the door related to the white-haired man. To Greeley he didn't seem the type to hand over his gun under any circumstances.

His doubt on that score was unfounded. When Greeley walked in it was to see six-shooters and gunbelts stacked neatly behind the bar, and the white-haired man was nowhere to be seen. Breathing a sigh of relief, wanting no further animosity between the Moore brothers and himself, Greeley was taking a final look around the bar when he saw the only man present wearing a gun. This was a rowdy, stockily built cowboy, who although not particularly tall was heavily muscled. Greeley noted that the man's drunken behaviour was accompanied by positive movements of his body that belied intoxication.

'That there's Big Dutch, Marshal,' a man who had the look of a trail boss volunteered. 'He sure ain't a man to be fooled with.'

'I never fool,' Greeley replied evenly as he went towards where Big Dutch was ending the snatch of a ballad he had been serenading his buddies with.

'Have we a problem here, Marshal?' the cowboy

asked with an exaggeratedly owlish look at Greeley.

'Not from where I'm standing, cowpoke. Just hand over your firearm.'

Taking in the bowed legs, well shaped for a horse-rider, an impediment for a fighting man, Greeley knew it was going to be easy. 'A bum you could beat without getting off your butt,' Uncle Elvir would have said. The cowboy's hands were too large, too gnarled to be fast with a gun.

His right hand patting the handle of his holstered gun, Big Dutch told Greeley, 'Y'know, I'm mighty fond of my little gun. So fond, that I reckon as how I'll keep her with me.'

Aware that the patting of the six-shooter was a ruse that could change into a draw if he made a move towards his own gun, Greeley did nothing for a moment. He could draw and kill the man before he could get anywhere near clearing leather. But that wasn't what he wanted. Bravado didn't call for a death sentence, and Greeley's ambitions would be annihilated by a reputation as a ruthless killer.

Big Dutch was continuing to pat his .45, eyes never leaving Greeley, who gave nothing away in either his eyes or his facial expression as he made his move. Left hand snaking out to grab the cowboy's wrist, Greeley pulled hard to bring Big Dutch forwards on to a crushing right-hand punch to the jaw.

The power of the punch yanked the cowboy's wrist from Greeley's grasp, sending him flying horizontally across the room like some type of human missile. The bar stopped the flight of Big Dutch, his head hitting the hard mahogany with a sickening thud before he flopped to the floor.

Striding over, Greeley flicked the inert cowboy's gun from its holster. Unbuckling the gunbelt, he pulled it off, and was straightening up to pass both to the bartender when something about the way Big Dutch was lying had him pause.

Dropping to one knee, Greeley briefly examined the cowboy. Lifting his head he saw Bob Marlin standing a few feet away, awe-struck. Greeley said crisply, 'Fetch the doctor, Bob.'

There was total silence as Greeley stood upright. There was no movement apart from when the two Moore brothers hurried out of their office and came over to stand a little way off, saying nothing.

Bob Marlin came back just ahead of the doctor, a small man who wore a bowler hat of a 'back East' style, and had grey whiskers that stuck out wirily from the sides of his face. With one arthritic leg staying straight out, the doctor lowered himself beside Big Dutch by folding his mobile leg in under himself in a peculiar way.

'Marshal!' he called after about half a minute.

'Yes, Doc?'

'His goddarned head's broke, neck's broke, and I'd bet my little woman's two gold teeth that his goddarned back's broke. You sent for the wrong man, Marshal. Ike Stevenson's building an extension on the baker's shop this very minute. Send your boy to get him so's he can make a pine box for this poor cuss.'

Greeley nodded to Bob Marlin, who stood with his mouth gaping open, eyes moving between Greeley and the man he had killed with a single blow. 'Go fetch the carpenter, boy.'

Bob went off in an awkward walk that was somehow made that way by his withered arm twisting at his body. Coming to Greeley's side, the doctor lifted his right hand in both of his, folding the fingers to turn the hand into a fist.

''T would be better to be kicked by a goddarned mule,' the doctor remarked with a sigh. Although used to death in its varied guises, he was keen to hurry away from this accidental one.

Standing behind Greeley, the trail-boss who had warned him about Big Dutch issued another quietly worded caution. 'He was with the Hash Knife outfit, Marshal. They ain't going to let this go.'

Making no reply, Greeley walked out into a street that had been strangely muted by the death of the man in the Cattleman's Cottage. It was the same everywhere, and when he took his first inspection of the night of the Golden Wheel, he found it as crowded as usual but the usually boisterous customers were so subdued and inactive that Hugh Hartman, the proprietor, had time for a conversation, although Greeley wasn't in the mood for talking.

'A bad business, Marshal, a real bad business,' Hartman said, alluding to the death of the cowboy. Being closer to seventy than sixty years of age, Hartman was set apart from Oaksworth's other saloon owners by at least a generation. A large man in an obese sense, his velvet vest and black silky jacket was stretched over a waistline that was so swollen by fat that it seemed to defy gravity. A cultured man with impeccable manners, his most striking feature was a pair of large brown eyes that held a kindness not expected in a man in his line of business.

'It wouldn't have happened if that cowpoke hadn't been breaking the law,' Greeley qualified his part in the death, while in no way excusing or defending himself.

Giving a wise nod, Rattan said, 'Of course, Marshal. I implied no criticism of you. You were doing your job, protecting this town and its good folk.'

Was that sarcasm, Greeley wondered? A man of Hartman's intelligence would have deduced that the cowboy had been killed by Greeley enforcing a rule to ruin trade at the Moore brothers' premises, and boost it at Richmond Coles's gambling house. It was rumoured that Hugh Hartman would be soon joining the Oaksworth town council. This was a prospect that worried Coles.

'I hadn't planned anything like it to happen,' Greeley said.

'You have no need to tell me that, Marshal. I have the greatest respect for you,' Hartman said. 'Oaksworth can't afford to be without you, Marshal. There are problems here, of course, but that is to be expected in any new town. We must hope that they are resolved for the best in Oaksworth.'

There was an ambiguity in what Hartman said. It was as if he was advising Greeley to stay clear of Richmond Coles and his machinations. But Hartman's had been a covert not an overt utterance, and Greeley, who had no time for anything other than forthright talking, had walked away without probing what the fat man might really have meant.

Reaching the American Playground he found it livelier than Hartman's place had been, but the death of Big Dutch had robbed the atmosphere of something vital there, too. Seeing Coles at the far end of the bar, operating one of the games himself, Greeley avoided him and went back out on to the street.

He felt morose as he continued his rounds. Having never before killed a man with his fists, he found that it had a far more dramatic effect on him than did shooting a man dead. Greeley reasoned that it was all a matter of intent. When you drew a gun it was to shoot to kill, while throwing a punch was done with the aim of stunning a man, rendering him temporarily incapable.

Passing the bank he saw two men loitering on the sidewalk outside. Walking over, Greeley found them to be two young cowboys who were taking a break between an evening of pleasure and riding out of town.

'Keep moving, boys,' he advised.

They both moved on without argument or question, and Greeley carried on his way, pausing outside Pat Brogan's saloon to watch a sudden flurry of activity further on at the door of the Cattleman's Cottage.

Coming out backwards, carrying one end of a long box, was Ike Stevenson, the busiest man in Oaksworth as a carpenter and part-time undertaker. A man who was a stranger to Greeley struggled with the other end of the box. Big Dutch would weigh pretty heavy. Fussing round them, obviously believing that Greeley had left him in charge, and determined to do his best, was Bob Marlin.

Glad to break away from the little parade of death, Greeley entered Pat Brogan's place, expecting it to be so quiet that his usual check would prove unnecessary. The crowd was thin enough for Pat Brogan and himself to see each other immediately he stepped inside the door. Their eyes met in a distant, silent exchange that ended with her getting a bottle and two glasses and walking to a vacant table in a corner. When he got there she had already filled one glass and was tipping the bottle towards the second.

'You look like a man who needs a drink,' she observed.

'I feel like a man who doesn't know what he wants,' he told her truthfully.

'I always prided myself on being able to help a man decide,' she said suggestively, 'but I guess this is a very different situation.'

Lifting the glass she pushed towards him, he drained it before answering, 'It is. Thanks.'

'I heard about it, Liam,' she said sympathetically, refilling his glass. 'As they say, you were only doing your job.'

He shook his head, wanting to keep to the truth. 'Not my job, Pat. I was doing what Richmond Coles wanted doing. Even that isn't correct, because I was doing it for myself.'

'So?' she asked, shrugging, the puffed shoulders of her red dress lifting, disturbing the long black hair.

'You keep the peace and look after your own interests at the same time. That sounds practical to me.'

'It's not what the townsfolk expect of their marshal.'

Pat Brogan snorted. 'I'm sure that it's not. They expect you to look after them and their property. They don't give a darn if you get shot in the middle of the night as long as they are safe. All for a few measly dollars a month. Do it your way, Liam. Most of them will suspect that you're feathering your own nest anyway.'

What she said didn't make any of it right, didn't square it with his conscience, but it helped. He liked being with her, was interested in what she had to say. Tonight she had gone easy on the cosmetics, and the real, lovely Pat Brogan showed through clearly. The eyes that looked excitingly into his were light grey rather than blue. Greeley made no objection when she refilled his glass again, and again. They sat together as hours passed by, their drinking slowing as a rapport built between them.

Most of the customers left without them noticing, and the bartender was clearing up, helped by one or two of the girls, while the others sat, weary from an evening of entertaining, of dancing with cowboys whose booted feet landed on theirs more often than they did the floor.

'You don't have to go back to your lonely bed tonight do you, Liam?' Pat Brogan asked, not looking at him as she did so.

At a total loss what to do, Greeley, in desperation, asked inside of his head for guidance, but Uncle Elvir must have been sleeping. So he did a sort of relaxation that let something deep inside of himself come up with an answer.

'No,' Liam Greeley heard his own voice say.

Hearing his name shouted out in the street awoke him.

There was enough light filtering through the curtains to tell him that sunrise wasn't far off. His name was called again, loudly, angrily, threateningly. Pat Brogan slept on, and Greeley got out of bed and into his clothes without disturbing her.

On the landing Greeley passed a girl saying farewell to a cowboy. Neither of them seemed to notice him as he went by and down the stairs. Checking that his Colt .45 was loaded, he went out into the greyness that a coming dawn was bringing to the blackness of night. His name was shouted again, coming from the direction of the new jail. Back against a building, peering carefully round the corner, Greeley saw three men lined up outside the jail. He surmised that they were from Big Dutch's outfit. Having ridden into town bent on revenge, they believed Greeley would be sleeping in the jail.

All three carried rifles, and he saw them engage in a short discussion as it came to them that he might not be inside the jail after all. The three of them split up. One was left to watch the jail, while the other two went their separate ways to seek him out.

Determined not to permit one killing lead to three more, Greeley made his way by a devious route to the rear door of the jail. Unlocking it, he went in, soft-footed. First going to the front door and noiselessly unlocking it, he made his way to the front window, peering out through a gap at the edge of the shutter. In the half light he could see the man with a rifle standing out in the street. Drawing his gun, Greeley used it to make a scraping noise with it against the shutter. When he saw the man outside become alert, he holstered his gun and slipped out of the back door.

Coming round the corner of the jail at the front, Greeley saw the man with the rifle pressed tightly up against the front wall, trying to peer in to discover what had made the noise. His back was to Greeley, who moved lightly up behind him to jab the muzzle of his gun hard into the man's spine.

Without saying a single word, Greeley reached with his spare hand to take the rifle from the hand of what was a slope-shouldered, unshaven boy who he guessed was less than twenty years old. Keeping the .45 digging into the youth's back, Greeley opened the door of the jail and pushed the man in ahead of him. Inside he unlocked the steel cage, shoved the boy in, and locked up again. Without either captive or captor having exchanged a word, Greeley went out.

It was lighter now, but he was able to stay hidden until he found a second man walking stealthily in the direction of the Grand Slam. Going round to the rear of the saloon, Greeley made his way up the side of it, staying in hiding, waiting round the corner, able to detect the footfalls of the advancing man. Timing it right, Greeley stepped out to front a tall, long-haired Texan. With the man too startled to bring the rifle into use, Greeley let go with a right-hand punch. Taking no chances this time, not wanting another tragedy, he grasped the man's shirt-front with his left hand. In this way, as his right fist connected solidly, breaking the man's jaw and knocking him unconscious, Greeley was able to lower him gently to the ground.

Taking the rifle with him, Greeley went off in search of the third and last man. He saw him, heading back towards the jail. Greeley needed to do some quick thinking. If the man got close enough to the jail to see that the companion he had left on guard there had gone, then he would be alerted to danger. Greeley could have brought him down with a shot from where he stood right then, but couldn't guarantee only wounding the man. Without realizing it, he had made a kind of a pact with himself to avoid further killing.

Going to the rear of the buildings once more, Greeley ran in the direction of the jail. It was fairly light now and he needed to plan something different. He considered opening the door of the jail then jumping the man when he came in to investigate. But the prisoner he had already locked up would be in a position to shout a warning to his buddy, so that idea had to be cancelled.

Moving out to the edge of a building, ahead of the slow-pacing man now, Greeley peeped round the corner into the street to see that he was coming along with his rifle held in readiness across his chest. He was older than the other two, and had a solidness of build that warned Greeley that he wouldn't be a pushover.

With no time to formulate an elaborate scheme, Greeley accepted that he had to take a chance. Keeping in tight to the corner of the building, he let the cowboy take two paces past in the street. Then Greeley stepped out, so close behind the man that he could see the individual hairs growing on the back of his neck. Although he had moved quietly, Greeley, who was about to draw his .45 to club the man with it from behind, realized that he had been heard. Spinning round, the man brought his rifle up, small eyes peering out of a battered face, looking round a twisted nose at Greeley. Not bothering to draw his gun, Greeley delivered a high-legged kick that whipped the rifle out of the man's hands and sent it flying through the air. With no time for considerate moves like holding the man's shirt to ease his fall, Greeley let go a tremendous right-hand punch.

As the knuckles were about to connect, the man showed fighting experience by moving his head a little to let the blow slip past. At the same time he took one step forward to slam a left and a right punch into Greeley's midriff. They were solid punches, but Greeley was protected by ridges of stomach muscles that he exercised regularly to keep in good shape. Taking the punches, Greeley clipped the man to the jaw with a jolting left hook, but when he tried to follow up with a right, the man swayed out of range and then ducked back closer to rock Greeley with a left and right of his own to the jaw.

Reminding himself that this wasn't a contest in New York, Greeley feinted with a right to the head. As the man took evasive action, Greeley kicked him hard in the shin, the toe of his boot cracking the bone. Following this with a knee in hard to the groin, Greeley then did deliver a perfect punch to the jaw. Prepared to drag the man into the jail when he went down, Greeley learned just how tough his opponent was. Having difficulty standing because of his damaged leg, and with his deepset eyes glazed, he stayed upright, nevertheless. Drawing his Colt, Greeley pistol-whipped the man, right and left across the temples, splitting the skin, drawing blood, knocking him unconscious.

Dragging the man inside the jail, Greeley locked him in and then walked back down the street to lift the still unconscious man lying in the dust up on to his shoulder. Carrying him effortlessly to the jail he tossed the man into the steel cage with the other two. The man with the split-open head was already regaining consciousness, blinking his eyes, glaring hatred at Greeley.

At last there was work for Bob Marlin to do, and Greeley hurried to the rooms at the rear of the Cattleman Cottage. He was hungry now and could really use some of Elizabeth Marlin's special coffee.

Dusting himself off outside, straightening his clothing, Greeley entered the Marlin quarters, anticipating the delight on Bobby face when he learned that he had prisoners to look after.

Opening the door of the kitchen, Greeley saw Bob and his sister sitting at the tables Then he felt a shock run through him from the top of his head to his toes. Sitting there with the Marlins, a tentative smile on her lips and tears brimming in her eyes, was Martha Jane Ackerman.

SIX

The meeting of the town council had first become argumentative when Thomas Bent, the general merchant, Merton Gaines, the barber, Hugh Hartman, the newest member of the council, and Bill Bradford the cattleman, had all joined James and Denis Moore in opposition to Richmond Coles's proposal that Liam Greeley be made mayor of the town. All of them were appalled by the motion, but Bill Bradford was outraged.

'I have all respect for Liam Greeley,' he roared at the Coles's faction on the council, 'and have had from the moment he arrived in Oaksworth, but what you are putting forward is ludicrous, Coles. Liam has filled the role of town marshal admirably, he is efficient and fearless, but I see the position of law officer as one that should be absolutely free from politics.'

'I second that,' James Moore said. 'What Bill Bradford is saying is inarguable.'

'Most definitely,' Denis Moore offered in support of his brother.

'I have to disagree,' Richmond Coles said decisively from where he sat beside Greeley, the man he had brought on to the council just ahead of Hugh Hartman, and whom he was now promoting. 'With the greatest respect, I have to say that you gentlemen are being extremely short-sighted. Due to the already referred to efficiency of our town marshal, and, I should add, his deputy, the town jail is now not just full, it is overcrowded.

'Ask yourselves, gentlemen, when is Oaksworth likely to see a judge? Not for a very long time. What do we do in the meantime, build a jail bigger than the town itself? No, you have the solution here and now. Marshal Greeley has shown us just how ably he can uphold the law. Who better, then, to be mayor and in a position to deal judicially with the miscreants apprehended in this town?'

The ring of logic that Coles's speech contained silenced the assembly for some time, and it was Merton Raines who was the first to speak. 'Perhaps I am on my own in this, but to me there has to be something unethical in having the man who arrests offenders also try and sentence them.'

'You're not on your own, Merton,' Bill Bradford stood to give emphasis to his words. An impressive figure, he was a man of common sense that, combined with a dedication to public duty, made whatever he said regarded highly. 'I have already stated the esteem in which I hold our town marshal, but I simply cannot go along with a plan that would have him become mayor, for exactly the reasons put forward by Councillor Raines.'

'Are you putting yourself forward as mayor, Councillor Bradford?' Coles smoothly enquired.

'Most definitely not,' Bradford said scornfully. 'I will judge a Longhorn with the best of them, Coles, but I'm danged if I'll sit in judgment on my fellow man.'

Greeley watched the argument swing back and forth. Becoming marshal had been a lift for him, but he saw the position of mayor as the first big step on his way to the top. Though aware of the strength of the opposition, he had faith in Coles's ability to win the day. Pat Brogan was already jokingly calling him mayor in private, but she said the joke had a base in premonition.

'At this stage, gentlemen, I think this debate merits an alternative suggestion,' Coles offered, but there were no takers.

'We need time,' James Moore grumbled.

'With the jail overflowing, Councillor Moore, time is one commodity that we don't have,' Coles replied. 'Now, shall we put this motion to the vote?'

With Greeley's abstention splitting the council evenly between the Coles faction and the non-Coles faction, the vote was a tie. The Moore brothers and their supporters were looking pleased with themselves, and Hugh Hartman said in his quiet way, 'That would seem to be it, gentlemen. This business must be deferred to another time.'

'That is not so.'

Richmond Coles had got to his feet to show that he intended to retake command of the situation, but Bill Bradford was ready for him.

'Leave it, Coles, leave it,' the cattleman advised. 'Even you can't do anything with a split vote.'

'It isn't a split vote, because Greeley hasn't yet contributed,' Coles said smugly.

'But that's asking a man to vote for himself,' James Moore objected in a manner that, for him, was fierce.

'Correction,' Coles said. 'Liam Greeley is a councillor and therefore entitled to vote. What say you, Councillor Greeley, are you for or against the motion?'

All eyes were fixed on the man who was at the crux of the contentious issue, but also held the casting vote. Feeling good, Greeley let them stew for some time. At last he gave the necessary one word answer. 'For.'

A short, stunned silence erupted into noisy movement as the disgusted Moore section of the council got angrily to their feet, putting their papers away, ready to leave. As they passed Greeley when they filed out they all glared at him. The most scathing glance of all, and the only one that affected him, came from Bill Bradford.

'Congratulations, Mr Mayor,' Coles smiled, shaking Greeley by the hand. 'Now, let's get down to business.'

For the remainder of that day, Greeley sat in a make-shift courtroom while Rafe Kennedy, aided by a suddenly self-important Bob Marlin, brought a long line of prisoners before him for sentencing. Greeley fined those who had the funds to pay up immediately, and slapped the remainder back in jail for sentences that varied from two to ten days.

That evening, when dinner was being eaten around the Marlin table, Bob could talk of nothing else but the business of the day and the personal part he had played in it.

Pleased to see her brother in such high spirits, Elizabeth managed to give Greeley a look that conveyed her gratitude. This surprised him, for Elizabeth had been increasingly avoiding communication with him since Martha Jane had arrived. To her credit, in Greeley's estimation, Elizabeth had concealed from Martha Jane just where, and with whom, he had spent the night of his girlfriend's arrival in Oaksworth. But in the ensuing days Martha Jane and Elizabeth had become close friends, with the former not noticing that there was any problem in her relationship with Greeley, while his disinterest in Martha Jane hadn't been missed by the astute Elizabeth.

Elizabeth tacitly blamed Greeley for this, but he didn't feel that he was personally responsible. In New York Martha Jane had been a girl to fill his whole world when he wasn't fighting. Believing her to be good for him, Uncle Elvir had encouraged what had been between the two of them. But so much had happened since, and life had taken such a dramatically rewarding turn that his relationship with Martha Jane had become flat and uninteresting for him.

She was smiling proudly at him now across the table.

'I can't believe it in so short a time, Liam. Just think of it, you're the mayor. What will I be when we marry, the mayoress . . . ?'

Martha Jane's face reddened as she realized what she was saying and she didn't end her sentence. An uncomfortable Elizabeth collected plates, scraping the leftovers from each on to one plate. Bob, ignorant of the undercurrents that were disturbing the other three, gave his opinion.

'You'll be the lady mayor,' he assured Martha Jane, eyes shining and his narrow face glowing as he looked at her. Bob had somehow merged the girl with Greeley so that she had become a part of his hero worship. In addition, he liked her a lot for herself.

'Better watch out for that Cad Pearse on your rounds tonight, Liam,' Bob Marlin said in a man-to-man way. It should have been a welcome change of subject, but it alarmed the two women.

Elizabeth shot a worried glance in Greeley's direction, and a frowning Martha Jane put her concern into words. 'Who is Cad Pearse, Liam?'

Before Greeley could give a suitably diluted, reassuring reply, Bob answered the question luridly. 'He's the fellow Liam beat over the head when he came into town to avenge the death of Big Dutch. He's real mean. Soon's Liam fined him ten dollars today, Cad Pearse started cursing like billy-o. Then he swore he'd get Liam if it's the last thing he does.'

'Is he dangerous, Liam?' Elizabeth put the question for both Martha Jane and herself, shelving for the moment her annoyance with Greeley for treating Martha Jane badly.

'They're all dangerous out there,' Greeley said as he drained his coffee cup.

'Might he get you, Liam?' Martha Jane's voice was trembling.

'He didn't the first time he tried,' Greeley said

laconically.

Even so, when he started his rounds he kept the possibility of being ambushed from the shadows by Pearse and his two companions on his list of self-preservation priorities. Going the full length of Main Street, he had decided to start at the American Playground. Although there was no change in the working relationship of Richmond Coles and himself, as becoming mayor that afternoon had shown, Greeley had of late detected a growing coldness in the saloon keeper's attitude towards him. Greeley couldn't put his finger on the reason for it, but it was there nevertheless, and it was perturbing. Greeley had enough to watch out for without having a disgruntled Coles at his back. This was on his mind when he was crossing the street ramp and a figure sitting with its back against the wall of the feed store shouted at him.

'Ho, bo. Tell me, ho, am I seeing things or is that New York Joe before me?'

Walking quickly to where the man squatted, Greeley found himself looking down at Illinois Dago. The hobo was in a bad way. Dirty and unshaven, he looked as if he was starving.

'Dago,' Greeley exclaimed in surprise, hunkering beside the tramp, not pleased to see him but linked to Illinois Dago by the still remembered hardships of recent times. 'I'm Marshal Greeley here, Dago, not Joe. Here.'

Reaching into his pocket Greeley took out three dollars and pressed them into the hobo's eager hand. 'Get yourself a meal and a stiff drink.'

'Very kind, very kind, bo,' Dago fought his way to his feet. 'But this is a hostile town, Joe . . . Marshal. I've just been thrown out from that joint.'

Illinois Dago had indicated the American Playground, and Greeley thought for a moment before saying, 'Can you see that place down there with the red light shining through the glass at the front?'

'Yo, bo.'

'Well, go round to the back door there and ask for Pat Brogan. Tell her I said to feed you and let you have a drink. But you pay her, mind.'

'I will, bo, I sure will,' Illinois Dago called back as he hurried off down the road.

'Dago!'

Greeley's shout halted the tramp, who stopped and turned, waiting impatiently.

'I want you out of town by sunrise.'

'Yo, bo,' Dago called back humbly before moving on, head down, and Greeley felt, guiltily, that the hobo was probably wondering what had happened to the 'code of the road'.

Standing watching his erstwhile travelling companion until the shadows of Main Street engulfed him, Greeley went into Coles's place. Business was good, the way it had been since Greeley had issued, and continued, the ban on wearing guns at the Cattleman's Cottage. Richmond Coles was at the bar, deep in conversation with a cattle-driver. The cow man drifted away when Greeley walked up.

'Ah, Liam,' Coles greeted him. 'I'm glad that you started here at my place. I have it on very good authority that there are three men waiting out there to get you tonight.'

'Then it's lucky I have a deputy to watch my back,' an ironic Greeley said. Since Rafe Kennedy had been deputized he had mostly been out of town on business for Coles. That had suited Greeley fine until tonight when he needed someone to watch his back.

'Come now, Liam,' Coles smiled in his facetious way. 'You should not be complaining. Tonight you should have the feeling of a town mayor.'

'How does a dead mayor feel?' Greeley asked sarcastically. 'Do you know where I can expect these three to be?'

'All I know is that it's not in here. Three men, that's my information. I'm told that you'll be able to recognize them as one has prominent scars across his forehead.'

'I put them there,' Greeley told Coles as he walked away from him, needing now to get moving, to find the three men and have the inevitable showdown over and done with.

They weren't in the Grand Slam, where business was quiet, or in the Golden Wheel, where the owner bought him a drink.

'Here's to our new mayor,' Hugh Hartman raised his glass.

'I didn't think that I'd be congratulated,' Greeley commented wrily.

Resting his elbows backwards on the bar to support his considerable bulk, Hartman gave an innocuous little smile. 'I can't say that I like the set-up, Liam, but that doesn't prevent me from liking you as a man.'

'The first may one day preclude the second,' he pointed out what seemed to him a distinct possibility.

'Very likely,' Hartman nodded, 'and when it does, Liam, you can rest assured that I will let you know my feelings in advance.'

Going out of the saloon, Greeley recognized that Hugh Hartman was one of the few straight people he had met in his lifetime. There was an unspoken bond between the two of them already. Neither Hartman nor anyone else could ever replace Uncle Elvir, but the ageing saloon proprietor was helping to fill the aching gap for Greeley.

There was only one place left for Cad Pearse and his two companions to be waiting, which was Pat Brogan's place. The no-gun rule at the Cattleman's Cottage would make them too conspicuous if they retained their firearms. So Greeley slowed as he neared Pat's saloon, finding the red glow of the light outside soothing as he relaxed his muscles, although it wasn't intended for that purpose.

He was standing manipulating his fingers the way Uncle Elvir had shown him, when the door of Brogan's shattered as someone was thrown out through it. A body hit the dust with a thud, but rolled over and sat up to face the two men who had ejected it.

'And stay out, dead-head,' one of the men shouted before they both went back into the saloon.

Aware who it was sitting in the dust before he got there, Greeley bent over, asking, 'Couldn't you get a meal and a drink without getting thrown out on your butt, Dago?'

'They're going to jump you in there, bo. They're waiting right now.'

Nodding, Greeley said. 'Thanks, Dago. There's three of them, one with a busted head.'

As Greeley helped the hobo to his feet, Illinois Dago spoke earnestly, 'There's those three, Joe, but they've sneaked four others in, too.'

'Thanks, Dago,' Greeley said, feelingly.

'The three are by the bar. You can't miss them, Joe, but they're only the decoy.'

'Do you know where the other four are?'

Dago nodded, shaking the dust of the street from his straggling hair as he did so. 'They're playing cards at a table away from the other three. You'll soon spot them. One of them, the feller furthest from you as you go in the door, is cockeyed.'

Thanking the hobo, Greeley patted him lightly on the back, flinching as he felt bones so devoid of flesh that they were threatening to break through the skin. As Illinois Dago walked off, hobbling a little from the impact with the street when he was thrown, Greeley realized that the hobo, though he would never have admitted it, had got himself thrown out purposely to be able to warn Greeley without arousing suspicion.

Standing for a moment, leaning against the hitching rail outside Brogan's, Greeley thought on how the courage and loyalty of a tramp contrasted with the wickedness of the men waiting for him inside. There were other things, too, that it was difficult to put together. The killing soon to come, and the outing Martha Jane had planned for her and himself tomorrow. Bob Marlin couldn't keep the secret to himself. He had told Greeley how his sister had helped by arranging the hire of a buggy and giving Martha Jane instructions on how to reach an idyllic spot beside the Smoky Hill River. The crippled boy had explained that an excited Martha Jane was going to tell him about the outing and the hamper of food she had lovingly packed, that night when he finished his rounds.

Since learning of the girl's plan Greeley had been dreading it. He had known that he would be bored, and that he wasn't a good enough actor to conceal the fact. But now, as he made his way in through the shattered door, that ride with Martha Jane had become very appealing.

Pearse and his two friends were by the bar, and Greeley saw the tremor of anticipation that ran through their bodies as he entered. Pat Brogan, at her usual place down the end of the bar, showed by the stiff way that she stood that she was aware of danger in the air. The three pushed away from the bar, standing side-by-side, far enough apart to have a clear draw, ready to challenge him.

Appearing to keep his eyes on the trio, Greeley spotted the four card players Illinois Dago had warned of. The light from one of two lamps almost immediately over the table reflected on the left eye of the man facing him, making it appear to be all white until Greeley could see an out of track pupil tucked in against the side of a hooked nose.

'Greeley!' Cad Pearse called, expecting the marshal to walk towards him, looking perturbed when Greeley walked at an angle across the floor. Reaching a wall, Greeley turned to face a mystified and worried trio who moved so that all three of them were once more facing him. Greeley now had a straight line between him and Pearse, and that line ran through the table at which the four men were sitting playing cards.

A hush had settled on the place now. Greeley's movements had warned the drinkers and the gamblers that something was about to happen. They didn't know what, and there was a shared fear of personal danger. Most uncomfortable of all were the four men who were now pretending, with difficulty, to be still interested in the card game.

With his left hand holding the back of a chair, Greeley's eyes flicked to a round, unoccupied table on his right, then upwards to the two lamps that illuminated the card table and most of that section of the saloon.

'You looking for me, Pearse?' he asked.

Not answering, Cad Pearse looked as if he wanted to ask the men at each side of him what was going on, but he couldn't afford to take his gaze off Greeley.

'Pearce, I'm wait . . .' Greeley started to say, but burst into action halfway through the sentence. With his left hand he tossed the chair up to shatter and extinguish one of the lights, while he drew and shot the other one out.

In the sudden and confused darkness, he kicked the table near him on to its side, dropping down behind it. Pearse, the two men with him, and the four at the table, were back-lit for Greeley by the lights behind the bar. His gun exploded, taking out three of the men at the table and bringing down the man flanking Pearse to the left. Pearse opened up then, and Greeley's shot went wide. But he was helped by Pearse accidentally hitting and killing his own remaining man at the table. The realization made Pearse stop firing.

Taking advantage of the short break in firing to reload, Greeley came up shooting. Pearse was running then, heading for the door. Standing, taking slow, deliberate aim, Greeley squeezed the trigger and Pearse spread his arms wide as if trying to fly as the bullet went into his back. He ran headlong into the door jamb, sticking there motionless, as if glued, before sliding into a heap on the floor.

Everyone in the saloon had been equally still, but then there was sudden movement. People coughing on the acrid cordite smell were lighting lamps to survey the damage. Bob Marlin came in through the door, right on cue, almost tripping over the body of Pearse, coming up to Greeley, the ultimate expression of adulation on his face. Others were crowding the doorway. Greeley could see the Moore brothers, Hugh Hartman, Jud Parkins, the young but oddly wizened owner of the Grand Slam, Richmond Coles and Bill Bradford looking in, before his attention was caught by a cowboy slumping wounded against the bar, blood pumping from a bullet wound in his thigh. This had been caused by a stray bullet from Greeley.

'Go to it, Bob,' he instructed. 'First get the doc to see to this cowpoke. Tell him that I'll pay. Then fetch Stevenson to take care of things.'

Walking slowly, a long, lean, gangling man with an Adam's apple that bobbed and leapt when he spoke, looked at the seven bodies and gave an incredulous gasp. 'A massacre!'

'Are you all right, Liam?' an anxious Pat Brogan came up to his side.

He assured her that he was, as the doctor came in the door to limp hurriedly to the side of the injured cowboy. Ike Stevenson arrived, armed with timber, nails, a hammer and two assistants.

It was some time, to Greeley's surprise, before Bob

Marlin returned, and the crippled boy immediately explained. 'I had to go home, Liam, else Martha Jane and Elizabeth would be worried when they heard about the shooting.'

Coming into the saloon, looking round at the bodies, Bill Bradford was obviously impressed by the fact that one man had faced such odds and survived. He took a step towards where Greeley stood by Pat Brogan, seemed to be about to say something, then changed his mind and walked off.

'Can I get you a drink now, or will you come back for it when your work is finished?' Pat Brogan asked, aware that he had one more round of Main Street before his duty as marshal would be complete for the night.

Feeling Bob Marlin's keen gaze on him, Greeley wasn't able to give the woman an immediate answer. Wanting to come back to her, needing to come back to her, he was tortured by the knowledge that Martha Jane was waiting to spring her surprise on him. The girl deserved better treatment than that he had afforded her since she had travelled from New York to join him. Greeley's wish was for things to be the same between Martha Jane and himself as they had been back East. But he knew that it could never be. He had travelled too many miles, met too many people, lived through too many experiences.

'I'm not sure that I'll be back,' he told Pat, gruffly.

Puzzled, she studied him for a moment before commenting. 'Things are moving too fast for you, Liam.'

'I can handle it,' he told her.

'I hope that you can, Liam,' she said quietly. 'Please be careful where Richmond Coles is concerned. I knew him at Abilene and before.'

'How well did you know him?' Greeley asked, uncertain whether he was experiencing suspicion or jealousy.

'Enough to know that he'll double-cross you,' she replied enigmatically.

The last of the bodies, that of Cad Pearse, was being carried out of the saloon in a hastily-constructed pine box. All reminders of the recent violence and death had been removed. Pat Brogan was right, things were happening too fast for him. Life was taking on a dream-like quality for Greeley and it worried him. He had to stay wide awake to survive.

'Coles is no better placed than I am, Pat,' he told her. 'We are both taking a chance on each other.'

She shook her black-haired head emphatically. 'Richmond Coles never takes a chance.'

Maybe, Greeley thought as he left her and walked out into the street, but only up until now. He watched the saloon owner carefully. If there was an increase in the coldness toward Greeley of late, then he would become suspicious. Coles boasted of his cunning, but Greeley had become convinced that he could match him for wits.

When he reached the American Playground an unusually anxious Coles hurried towards him. Kennedy was back in town, standing, as always, in the shadow of Richmond Coles.

'Have you finished for the night, Liam?'

'No,' Greeley answered, wondering what was ailing the saloon owner. 'I've to close the street down yet.'

'Rafe can take care of that,' Coles replied, gesturing for Kennedy to leave and start work. Taking Greeley by the elbow, applying pressure to take him towards the bar, an unusually subdued Coles said, 'I'll get you a drink, Liam.'

Across the room, sitting in his customary back-to-the-wall position, was the white-haired man. Greeley was aware that the man had seen him, but his eyes had flicked away now, ignoring the marshal. The appearances of the white-haired man in Oaksworth, and his disappearances, had at first intrigued Greeley, but now it was causing him concern. He was a dangerous man, and the more he thought about it the more Greeley felt there had been a veiled threat in the white-haired man's comment that he hadn't believed there were two men in the world who could beat Marion Clay to the draw.

'Do you know who that man is, the one over there with the white hair?' Greeley asked Coles.

'Forget him, whoever he is,' Coles tersely replied. 'We've got a problem, a big one. The Moores and the others have left the council, Liam. Bill Bradford is at the heart of it. Under him they're setting up some kind of citizens' committee.'

'Vigilantes?' Greeley checked, worriedly.

'They'd never get anyone to join them while your gun and your fists are in town,' Coles said with a pleased little chuckle, enjoying having Greeley's power on his side. Then he became deadly serious again. 'There's talk of them bringing Sam Kingsley in. He's the county sheriff.'

'Is he a problem, Richmond?'

'Not in the sense that he's likely to brace you,' Coles smiled again. 'Kingsley's knocking on in years and will know that he is no match for you, Liam. The problem is that he's the real law, and if we deal with him it will only mean someone else being sent in behind him.'

'So?'

Finishing his drink, Coles shifted his feet, nervously, Greeley was quick to notice. When he spoke the old self-confidence that so often strayed into arrogance was absent. 'I haven't made up my mind what to do. Leave it with me, Liam.'

Leaving the saloon, Greeley met Kennedy doing a fairly brisk walk back up Main Street, and asked him, 'Any problems?'

'Nothing serious,' Kennedy shrugged, as reluctant as

ever to meet his eyes, or anyone else's for that matter. 'Some crazy buffalo hunter didn't want to give up his gun in the Cattleman's Cottage. He decided to shoot up the place instead.'

'You put him in the jailhouse?'

'Nope, just run him out of town,' Kennedy said before walking on.

His unwanted deputy could handle himself, Greeley would grant him that, but it still didn't make him like having the fellow around. Kennedy was sly and untrustworthy, but, like everything else he faced in Oaksworth, Greeley was confident of being able to handle him.

Walking on through a Main Street that was starting a night's slumber, Greeley saw a familiar, twisted figure at the far end. Standing at the mouth of the side lane leading to the restaurant and Marlin home at the rear of the Cattleman's Cottage, crippled Bob was trying to give the impression that he wasn't waiting for Greeley. The boy failed, as his intention was obvious.

Nearing the Pat Brogan saloon Greeley mentally checked out two half-drunken cowboys sitting outside, talking loudly to each other in a maudlin manner, the pair of them harmless. Walking on, knowing that it wasn't only Bob Marlin waiting expectantly for him, Greeley found himself anticipating with pleasure a peaceful day beside the river with Martha Jane.

In the shadow of the doorway, the door having been repaired by Ike Stevenson on what must have been one of his busiest nights, someone stood. A wary Greeley let his right hand hover over his .45. But then his name was called in the melodious voice of Pat Brogan.

His hesitation was brief. Turning right, he walked towards the saloon and the waiting woman. As he entered the door, Greeley turned to see Bob Marlin standing facing him squarely. Then the crippled boy turned and ran homewards through the night.

SEVEN

There was a deceptive air of peacefulness to Oaksworth just after sunrise. As Greeley left Pat Brogan's place to head for the Marlins' home there was nothing moving other than a teamster's wagon in the far distance. There was nothing even to hint at the angry divisions bubbling just below the surface. At the root of it all was greed and the lust for power. Acknowledging that he was part of the latter, and possibly to some extent the former, Greeley found that it didn't trouble him. Some short while ago it would have, but he had recently passed some kind of watershed where conscience was concerned. It would have been easy enough to blame the influence of Richmond Coles, but Greeley was still honest enough to admit to himself that, when it came down to basics, the main fault lay with himself desperately wanting to be somebody.

When he went in it was to find the two women and Bob sitting at the table. At his entrance Martha Jane jumped to her feet and ran out of the room, but she hadn't gone quickly enough to prevent Greeley from seeing that she was crying, and had been for some time. Guilt knifed through him as he saw the hamper off to one side, tipped over and with the previously lovingly packed contents spilling out.

Standing, Elizabeth Marlin looked him straight in the

eye. 'You're no longer welcome here. Please collect your things and leave.'

Staggered by this, Greeley looked at her brother. The crippled boy had also stood, his divided loyalties showing on his face. Deciding to sit on the fence until the air cleared, Bob Marlin remained silent.

But when Greeley had packed his few belongings and went out of the door, without any sight of Martha Jane, and with Elizabeth not having uttered another word, the boy followed. Greeley was prepared to walk away, but Bob ran round to stand in front of him, blocking his way. Even in the upsetting circumstances, Greeley noticed the fear in the crippled boy, and admired him for overcoming it. Only the stupid found being brave easy.

'You going to Pat Brogan's?' Bob Marlin asked in an accusatory tone.

That had been Greeley's plan before stepping out into the street, but he had cancelled it out before the boy had asked his question. Recognizing that he had brought this upon himself, Greeley bitterly regretted having done so. The animosity of a section of the townsfolk against him, which was a product of his ambition, was of no great consequence to Greeley. But he had become extremely fond of Elizabeth and Bob Marlin, and was keenly aware that Martha Jane was too good a person to deserve being hurt by him. Yet the more mature Pat Brogan, with her unfathomable depth of character, was so much more interesting and exhilarating to be with.

'I'll guess that I'll bunk down at the jail for a time,' he told Bob.

'I'll walk with you, as I've got to feed the prisoners,' Bob Marlin said, speaking no more as he fell in at Greeley's side.

Neither was there any conversation at the jail, although Greeley did try. Each time there was no response from the boy, and Greeley was conscious of how much pain it gave Bob not to speak to man he idolized.

Greeley was pondering on a way to ease things for the crippled boy when a delegation made up of the two Moore brothers, Bill Bradford and Hugh Hartman arrived at the jail. James Moore had obviously been appointed as spokesman.

'I won't beat about the bush, Greeley . . .' he started to say, but Greeley raised a hand to stop him.

'You finished your chores here, Bob?' he asked the boy, and when he received a curt nod in reply he added, 'Off you go then. I'll see you back here at dinnertime.'

As the crippled boy went out of the door, Greeley beckoned his little group of visitors into a part of the L-shaped building that was out of earshot of the men locked in the steel cages. As far as he knew they were a nondescript bunch, but there could be someone there able to carry a tale of what he had overheard to the wrong quarter

'Now,' Greeley invited Moore to continue.

'I won't beat about the bush, but give it to you straight, Greeley,' a sombre James Moore said.

'No sense in shillyshallying,' his brother said.

'Leave it to James, Denis,' Bradford advised.

'Yes, leave it to me,' James Moore said, ill at ease.

'Yes, I'll leave it to you, brother,' Denis Moore said unnecessarily.

'Denis . . .' Bradford said warningly.

Waiting to be certain that he wouldn't be interrupted again, James Moore delivered his message. 'You will have heard that a number of us have left the town council to form our own committee. We have come here to make this offer once, and once only, Greeley. You can from this moment onwards join us under the leadership of Bill Bradford. Should you not accept our offer, then we must immediately assume that you choose to remain with the town council.'

'Which has been hog-tied by Richmond Coles,'

Bradford made clear the low regard in which they held the council.

'You've sprung this on me, gentlemen,' Greeley replied. 'I need time to consider your offer.'

'I've already firmly stated that your answer is required right now,' James Moore reminded him. 'If you say yes, then we will welcome you as the law officer in Oaksworth, a law officer answerable to the citizens' committee we have formed.'

'If you do not come with us,' a determined Bill Bradford informed him, 'then I intend to hold a meeting to gather all the right-thinking people in this town, following which the sheriff of this county will be called in to administer the law correctly in Oaksworth.'

'If I should accept, I would assume that it would be on certain terms, your terms,' Greeley said.

'Not terms, exactly, but we would expect certain things to be done,' James Moore tried to make the offer sound reasonable.

'Like the ban on wearing guns being lifted from your place?' Greeley suggested with a faint smile. But his smile faded when James Moore gave a negative shake of his head.

'Not at all. But we would anticipate it being extended to all other saloons and gaming houses in town.'

'Except for the American Playground,' Bradford came in to give Greeley another surprise.

'Why not the American Playground?' he raised an eyebrow, prepared for anything.

'Because you will be closing it down.' Hugh Hartman spoke for the first time since the citizens' delegation had arrived at the jail.

A dubious Greeley said, 'I have no reason to close down the place.'

'We'll find a reason,' James Moore assured him.

That was the point at which Greeley made his

decision. These supposedly upright representatives of the town might not be as criminally ruthless as Richmond Coles, but they had just admitted to being unprincipled. He felt that the departed Uncle Elvir was supporting him fully when he gave them his answer.

'I was made marshal by the town council, gentlemen, so it would seem unwise to change my allegiance.'

'I'm sure that I speak for us all when I say that your decision is regretted,' James Moore said unhappily.

'We regret it very much,' said his brother.

'I feel that you may well regret it,' Bradford told Greeley.

Shrugging, Greeley said, 'We all have to bear responsibility for our own actions and decisions.'

'When I first made your acquaintance, Liam, when you put on that excellent show against Cherokee Dave, I would never have believed that I would find you in your present circumstances,' Bill Bradford said in genuine sorrow.

'Nevertheless, Bill,' James Moore pointed out to his colleague, 'we have made our offer and it has been rejected. We must go now, as there is much to do.'

Bradford nodded, then addressed Greeley. 'When we leave here I shall be spreading the word that the citizens' committee is holding an important meeting in the Cattleman's Cottage in one hour's time. You are welcome to attend, Liam, but not in your capacity as town marshal.'

'I might come along,' Greeley said, not qualifying whether he planned to attend as a marshal or simply as a private citizen.

When they had gone and he felt very much alone in the jail, the prisoners meaning nothing to him, Greeley had his first misgiving since coming to Oaksworth. From a personal viewpoint he had alienated the three most important people in his life. Pat Brogan was great to be with, but there was something about her that prevented Greeley becoming close to her, he guessed in a spiritual sense, as he was to the Marlins and Martha Jane. Yet he had already forsaken the simple purity of Martha Jane for the hard, brazen, yet powerfully magnetic Pat Brogan.

But he had hopes, high hopes, of being able to sort out his private life although the split between the businessmen of Oaksworth had become a daunting thing. At the moment, although he had turned down the offer presented by James Moore, Greeley felt that he was still straddling the divide, with a foot still in each of the two camps.

Deciding to postpone any planning until he had heard what was said at the citizens' committee meeting, he left the jail and was walking in the direction of the Cattleman's Cottage when a single shot rang out up ahead.

Greeley quickened his pace as the sounds of shouting and screaming came from Main Street. Then three people came running round the corner up ahead, obviously heading for the jail until they saw him and veered his way. In front was Clem Evans, a young man who had recently arrived in Oaksworth to open a printer's shop. Despite being an academic rather than a physical hard man, Evans was both articulate and courageous, Greeley had noticed. The printer would make a valuable contribution to the citizens' committee. A few more like Evans behind the forceful Bill Bradford and the committee would really be something to be reckoned with.

But now Clem Evans had shed his usual composure as he ran up to Greeley, red of face, agitated and sweating as he gasped out, 'You have an arrest to make, Marshal. Your deputy has just shot and killed Bill Bradford in the street.'

Shaken by this, Greeley ran with Evans and the other two as they turned and headed back for Main Street.

Reaching where a crowd had gathered, Greeley pushed through and dropped to one knee beside the prone Bradford. The cattleman had been drilled through the heart, dying instantly. Having liked and respected the man who had given him his first start in this town, Greeley felt a sorrow at his death that amounted to something like grief. He stood and asked what had happened, and everyone around him answered at the same time.

'You tell me,' Greeley pointed at Clem Evans.

'It was your deputy, Kennedy, Marshal. He'd been out here in the street taking firearms off everyone going to the meeting at the Cottage,' the printer replied, pointing to a pile of gunbelts and firearms stacked in the street, apparently by Rafe Kennedy. 'Bill Bradford said he wasn't carrying a gun. He was opening his coat to prove this, when your deputy shot him down.'

'That's true,' a chorus of voices shouted.

'Bradford wasn't armed, Marshal,' someone called, and his assertion was taken up by other people.

Three men came pushing forwards. At first Greeley took them to be strangers, cowboys off the trail, but then he remembered seeing them in the American Playground the previous night. At that time he had placed them as men whose guns were for hire. He still had that opinion now as they came up.

'We were standing just over yonder,' said one, dark enough to have either Indian or Mexican blood in this veins, 'and we saw it all. That joker lying there went for a gun, sure 'nuff. If your deputy hadn't fired, Marshal, he'd have been dead himself.'

'Then where's the gun, mister?' Evans challenged the hard-faced man.

The three men made a pretence of studying the ground around the body, and showed exaggerated surprise at not seeing a weapon lying there. The dark-skinned man said, 'It was lying there, Marshal, right where the dead *hombre* dropped it. I guess one of these folks hereabout picked it up and hid it away.'

'This is nonsense, Marshal,' Clem Evans protested from where he stood with his pretty wife holding his arm. 'He might be your deputy, but he should be arrested.'

'He will be,' Greeley promised, 'and held until we find out the truth. If there was no gun, then Kennedy will stand before a judge on trial for murder.'

'There was no gun,' Evans led a concerted cry of protest.

Seeing Richmond Coles observing from the outer edge of the crowd, Greeley called, 'Where is Kennedy?'

'He rode out of town straight after the shooting, Marshal,' Coles shouted back.

'Then get after him, Marshal,' Clem Evans urged.

'I'm Marshal in Oaksworth, and have no jurisdiction outside of the town limits,' Greeley pointed out. Certain that Bill Bradford had been unarmed, Greeley intended to bring Rafe Kennedy to justice or, preferably, kill him, but to do so outside town was likely to have him arrested for murder.

'So you're going to let him get away?' an incredulous Clem Evans cried, bringing an eruption of verbalized anger from the crowd.

'When Kennedy comes back into town, I'll have him,' Greeley said.

'What if he doesn't come back?' an irate James Moore shouted.

'He'll be back,' Greeley said assuredly, seeing Ike Stevenson in the crowd and gesturing for him to come forwards. 'Right now the priority is to see that this man gets the burial he deserves. Do what you have to do, Stevenson, and let me have the bill.'

There was angry muttering behind Greeley as he walked away. Impatience led to mistakes, often fatal errors, and he was not swayed by the folks of

Oaksworth's demands for instant justice. He was content to bide his time. One day Rafe Kennedy would be his. It was a day that Liam Greeley looked forward to with relish.

It was late afternoon before he realized that he had become so used to regular meals at the Marlins' home that he hadn't eaten all day. He went out, securing the jail door behind him, and going to Pat Brogan's place, which was empty at that time of day. Asking no questions, she made him a meal. She seemed to get pleasure from watching him enjoy the food, which reminded him of the homesteader's wife. That seemed so long ago now that it could have been another lifetime.

'I should have warned you before about Richmond Coles, Liam,' she said suddenly and seriously as they sat drinking together when he had finished eating.

'You've told me several times that he's dangerous,' Greeley told her, detached and uninterested.

'There's more to it than that, Liam,' she said. 'Me and him used to be er . . . together. He's a strange, jealous man, and he just can't accept that there is nothing between us any more.'

Not commenting, Greeley stood, thanked her for the meal and walked out, aware of her anxiety as she watched him go. This explained Coles's increasing coolness towards Greeley despite their joint plan working well. The saloon owner's displeasure at Greeley's relationship with Pat Brogan didn't worry him in the slightest, but the edge of his feelings for Pat had been blunted by learning that she had once been Richmond Coles's woman. Greeley was unhappy as he made his way back to the jail, from where he would go out on his rounds, and then come back to and spend the night there in abject loneliness.

Going inside, Greeley was prevented from closing the door behind him as Bob Marlin, having come running up in panic, collided with it.

'You have to come, Liam,' the crippled boy choked out his words breathlessly. 'They're getting ready to go.'

Letting the boy in, closing the door, Greeley said, 'Calm down, boy. Who is getting ready to go, and where are they going?'

'A posse,' the crippled lad gasped. 'They're getting ready to go after Kennedy.'

Hurrying to open the gun cupboard, Greeley took out a sawn-off shotgun and loaded it with buckshot. 'Who's leading the posse, Bob?'

Greeley knew the answer to his question before Bob Marlin replied. 'Clem Evans.'

Walking unhurriedly down to Main Street, Bob Marlin at his side, Greeley carried the shotgun on his shoulder. He found the would-be posse assembled outside the bank, not yet mounted up, packing supplies into saddle-bags, so intent on their task that they didn't notice that the marshal had arrived until he climbed up on to the boardwalk and spoke.

'What's going on here, you men?'

'We've formed a posse, Marshal,' Evans said, coming forward to stand, legs apart, looking up at Greeley. 'We're going out to get Kennedy.'

'Not so,' Greeley shook his head as he lowered his shotgun from his shoulder. 'None of you are leaving town.'

'What's your objection, Marshal, seeing as you aren't doing the job yourself?' Evans asked.

'This isn't a posse, it's a lynch mob,' Greeley answered.

'It's no more'n that killer Kennedy deserves.'

'Who are you, Evans, to decide who deserves what?'

Evans retorted angrily, 'I could ask you the same question, Greeley. But it don't matter. You can't stop all of us from going.'

'I can stop you, and enough of the others to make everyone change their mind,' Greeley said flatly, giving the sawn-off shotgun a menacing twitch. He was rewarded by seeing the resolve dwindle in most of the posse.

'The thing is, Marshal,' Evans said quietly, moving closer to Greeley but keeping in the shadow cast by his horse, 'I've got a Navy Colt aimed at your gut right now.'

'I guess that's a pretty good argument,' a resigned Greeley said, lowering his shotgun so that it no longer threatened anyone. He continued talking as he took a couple of steps, his wide shoulders slumped. 'I didn't reckon on no . . .'

Using one of his favourite tricks by going into action in mid sentence, Greeley snaked out his left hand to pluck Evans's gun out of his hand, dropping it to the ground, then backhanding Evans, hard, with the same hand in one blindingly swift movement. The meaty smack of Greeley's hand against Evans's face filled the street for a moment, and the other members of the posse watched in horror as Evans, who had been sent spinning by the blow along the side of his horse, did a leg-buckling fall to the ground, blood pumping from his nose and gushing from his mouth as Greeley lifted the sawn-off shotgun and had them all covered once more.

It was Bob Marlin, who had been standing a little way off, who called out, alerting the posse that something else was happening. 'Liam, look!'

'I see him, Bob,' Greeley called to the boy as, mystified, he watched Rafe Kennedy ride slowly into town.

The deputy came on at a steady trot, saluting Coles with a raised hand as he came out of the door of his saloon. He came riding on to finally stop his horse a little way away, sideways to the posse and Greeley. Some of the men had been tending to Evans, bringing him up to his feet and holding him there because he was still unconscious. As they saw who the newcomer was they lost interest in their friend, dropping him back down in the dust.

'What goes, Kennedy?' Greeley called.

'I've ridden back into town to tell it just how it was, Marshal,' Kennedy, still in the saddle, replied. 'That man drew first.'

'Who do you figure on telling, Kennedy?'

'You, of course, Marshal who else?'

'I'm planning on you telling it to the judge, Kennedy,' Greeley said, stepping down from the sidewalk and walking towards Bob Marlin.

Placing the sawn-off shotgun in the boy's good arm, aiming it at the crowd of waiting men, among whom Clem Evans was now climbing groggily to his feet, putting Bob's finger in through the guard and round the trigger, he gave instructions.

'If one of them as much as blinks too hard, Bob, let them have it.'

Leaving the crippled boy brightly alert and full of self-importance, Greeley walked slowly over to where Kennedy sat relaxed on his horse. Richmond Coles had now come right out of his place, and he called a reminder across to the Marshal. 'Remember who you are, Greeley.'

'It's best that you remember who I am, Coles,' Greeley said as he stopped walking and stood looking up at Kennedy. 'Get down, Kennedy. This side of your horse and keep your hands high.'

Kennedy didn't move. 'I don't reckon I'll be doing as you say, Marshal. It's like this, see. I don't agree with you at all about me going before a judge.'

As he stood waiting, Greeley was working it out in his head. This was the cunning that Coles had boasted of. He was using Kennedy and was prepared to sacrifice him, although Kennedy couldn't know this.

Coles had feared the citizens' committee and had slowed down its growth by having Kennedy kill Bradford. Now he had somehow persuaded Kennedy to come back into town, fully aware that Greeley would arrest him. The incensed folk of Oaksworth would then attack the jail, probably burning it to the ground, and lynch Kennedy. The citizens' committee would then be looked upon as totally lawless, and Richmond Coles would be seen as the man who restored law and order to the town. Greeley decided to go along with it for as long as it benefited him.

'I guess the next move is yours, Marshal,' Kennedy said.

'You're making it easy for me, Kennedy,' Greeley smiled, hand hovering above his .45, relying on his intuition that told him Coles didn't want Kennedy dead right then.

'Hold it, hold it,' Richmond Coles said urgently, coming forwards fast while keeping a wary eye on the gun hands of both Greeley and Kennedy.

In the tension that had built up, and the silence apart from an infrequently spoken, brief sentence, Kennedy's horse had been lulled into a kind of trance. Coles's sudden dash forwards brought it out of its half-sleep and straight into a panic. With a wild screech the horse reared up, causing Richmond Coles to fall backwards as he tried to avoid its slashing front hooves. Kennedy was about to grab the saddle horn when Greeley stepped forward to pull his left foot out of the stirrup. Getting both hands under the sole of Kennedy's boot, Greeley threw him upwards, watching him go flying over the horse.

By catching hold of its head, Greeley swung himself round to the other side of Kennedy's horse. He got there as Kennedy, his reflexes working well, hit the ground while drawing his gun at the same time. Kneeling, he was bringing the gun up to bear on

Greeley. With the grace of a dancer, Greeley shot his left foot forward to crack against Kennedy's wrist sending the .45 he had held spinning through the air. Then, using that foot as a pivot, he kicked out with his right to catch Kennedy in the head and knock him violently on to his back in the dust.

Stooping to catch hold of Kennedy by one leg and an arm, Greeley threw him up and across the saddle of his own horse. Leading the animal round, Greeley reclaimed the sawn-off shotgun from Bob Marlin.

'Go to your homes, you people,' he told the crowd, then turned to Coles who had come up with the intention of walking with him. 'You go on back to your place, Coles.'

'As I told you earlier, Greeley, don't get above yourself,' Coles warned in a low voice.

Not replying, Greeley led the horse off towards the jail, the crippled boy at his side.

'I'll guard the jail with that shotgun tonight, Liam,' Marlin said, savouring the idea. 'Those men are all riled up and they'll want to get Kennedy.'

'You're right, boy,' Greeley nodded, 'about them likely to come after Kennedy, but you're wrong about you staying at the jail tonight.'

'Aawwwh ' Bob Marlin complained, reminding Greeley, 'I'm the jailer, remember, Liam. You'll need help if they come after Kennedy.'

'I'll need more help if your sister comes after me,' Greeley commented wryly.

'I'm not a kid.'

'To Elizabeth you are,' Greeley told him as they reached the jail and he lifted Kennedy from where he lay draped across the saddle.

Kennedy was stirring, back on the fringe of consciousness. The left side of his face had swollen up and was a mottled purplish colour. The bruising was worse because the skin hadn't broken to permit bleeding. There was, Greeley noticed, a trickle of blood seeping from the man's ear.

He doubted that the men who had aimed to form a posse would come after Kennedy that night. Not naturally fighting men they would need time to talk and scheme their next move. The fact that Clem Evans wouldn't be feeling too good for a while deprived them of a leader, so as Greeley half rolled, half threw the groaning Kennedy into a cage and locked him in, he felt confident that his sleep wouldn't be disturbed when he bedded down in the jailhouse for the first time. There was a possibility that Coles would somehow stir things up, but, crafty though the saloon owner was, he would have difficulty in getting an enraged mob together quickly.

'Thanks for your help down there, Bob,' Greeley said to the boy, noting how pleased the lad was to have actually been trusted to hold a gun on the posse. 'You go home now. There'll be no trouble here tonight.'

'If you're sure,' the boy said doubtfully, but then he left when Greeley lost interest in him and went over to sit on a bunk.

Greeley hadn't expected things to become so complicated. It had become so because Coles had acted rashly. The two separate factions in the town had become too widely opposed too soon. Much now depended on how what was left of the citizens' committee reorganized or fell apart. Whatever happened, it would be speeded up by Kennedy's arrest.

Having pondered on this, Greeley made an instant decision. He wasn't going to barricade himself in the jail to protect Kennedy as his prisoner. If they wanted the man, then they could come and get him.

Tonight Greeley would do his rounds as usual. His first call, he thought as he stood, would be at Pat Brogan's for a much needed meal.

EIGHT

Any chance of the citizens' committee becoming a force to be reckoned with had died with Bill Bradford. When, three days after arresting him, Greeley had released Rafe Kennedy through 'lack of evidence' there had been no organized protest. There were reports of some disgruntled mutterings in various parts of the town, but there were no public objections despite Greeley having reinstated Kennedy as his deputy. Both the release and reinstatement of Kennedy had been at the behest of Richmond Coles, and Greeley had willingly complied because the saloon owner and himself had settled their differences without actually confronting or discussing them. Greeley could trace the new relationship to the afternoon when Coles had asked him to walk to the railway yard with him. Once there, Coles had outlined what had the appearance of dreams but had become solid projects. The saloon owner had dropped his animosity towards Greeley, yet Greeley, who had seen Martha Jane only from a distance since the morning Elizabeth Marlin had asked him to move out, had become closer than ever towards Pat Brogan.

As he had stood beside Coles listening to his plans, Greeley had for the first time recognized what a clever businessman Coles really was. Before moving to Oaksworth he had arranged massive financial backing.

All his backers asked of Richmond Coles was that he arrange the right circumstances for their investment, and he was doing just that.

'There has to be progress, Liam,' he had said, watching the age-old, dusty, noisy driving of cattle going on all around them. 'Imaginative progress that requires as much courage, possibly more, than gun-fighting. Look at what's happening before you, Liam. The trail drivers want the best price for all their hard work, while the shipping agents want to make sure that they are rewarded for their expertise. So they haggle, and if the price isn't right they hold back from selling. All the time the cattle cost money to feed, while at the same time the beef probably loses weight.

'Oaksworth is thriving and becoming wealthier by the day, Liam, but it won't last. I made two fortunes for myself in Abilene, but now that town's deader than a coyote's supper. This place won't be booming much longer. Nobody will notice it happening, but one day there'll be a school, a church, and boring respectability here. But I've got my sights set on better things and, like I said, Liam, I'd like to take you with me.'

Greeley had squinted against the afternoon sun while considering asking just how Coles intended to change what appeared to be the natural rise and fall sequence of the West, when the saloon owner had started to speak again, saying that the answer lay in having the beef killed here, frozen, then sent back east in refrigerator cars.

'We'll be the middlemen, Liam, selling direct from the ranch to the consumer,' Coles had said, the light of a true visionary in his eyes as he pointed to an area of flatland on the far side of the pens. 'I already have an option on that land. It is where a packing plant will be built. We'll have a blood-drying machine, and markets for by-products such as fertilizer. Stay with me, Liam, and you'll be a prosperous businessman and mayor of a proper town.'

It had made sound sense and Greeley had been impressed. He could understand Coles's claim that the saloons and gambling dens of a cow town were so shortlived that they were only useful for making money for investing in more lasting, stable businesses.

Thinking about this now as he began his nightly rounds of Main Street, Greeley stepped into the Cattleman's Cottage, exchanging curt nods with the two Moore brothers. Their relationship was still very much an aloof one.

When he came back out on the street, Bob Marlin was, as always, lurking not far away, fretting because Greeley would not allow him to walk with him because of the danger involved. The crippled boy still worked at the jail, feeding the prisoners and keeping the place clean. Through Greeley he had, without any difficulty, secured a contract for his sister to provide the meals for the men locked up in the jail. Very often when with Greeley, Bob would try to steer the conversation into talk of Martha Jane and his sister. But Greeley always took evasive action. He found himself desperately wanting to hear news of Martha Jane, how she was getting along, but he judged himself unworthy of even such remote contact with the New York girl. It was common knowledge that she was helping out Elizabeth in the restaurant, but that was all that Greeley knew about her present circumstances.

That evening he judged that the town was at its busiest ever. He checked out the Grand Slam, where business was brisk, noisy but not threatening in any way. In the Golden Wheel Greeley felt a little jolt as he spotted the white-haired man, alone as usual, sitting in a corner that protected him on three sides. Taking a casual, alert stroll around the place, taking a glance at gaming tables and the men at them as he went, Greeley attempted to make his proximity to the white-haired man look accidental.

But he didn't fool the man. 'Do I worry you, Marshal?'

'Not worry, exactly,' Greeley said, standing by the table, studying the man who was so odd-looking from the colour and length of his hair. 'I just make a note of everyone who wears a gun and has a look of being able to use it.'

'In your job it pays to know their business,' the white-haired man nodded his agreement.

'It helps to guarantee a tomorrow.'

'I have too many yesterdays for me to be interested in a tomorrow, Marshal,' the man said.

That statement had to remain a puzzle to Greeley, as Hugh Hartman was beckoning him over. The saloon owner had a bottle and two glasses on a table behind which he had wedged his huge bulk. 'I'd like a word, Liam. Join me in a drink.'

Sitting, Greeley waited for his glass to be filled, raised it in a silent toast, then drank as Hartman studied him before speaking. 'The lull before the storm, do you think, Marshal?'

'I don't understand,' Greeley replied as his glass was refilled.

'Here in Oaksworth,' Hugh Hartman said, offering Greeley a cigar, lighting one for himself when the marshal refused. 'The town is booming, Liam. There's money to burn here. Right now there is some kind of truce, but Oaksworth will soon have to decide whether it wishes to go the citizens' committee way into respectability, or the Richmond Coles way into lawlessness and possible anarchy.'

'I thought that the citizens' committee had been disbanded.'

'Definitely not, Liam. I confess that the loss of Bill Bradford could have dealt us a finishing blow, but we have recovered and grow stronger by the day. Many new traders and merchants, all with a long-term view of the town, have moved here and have joined us.'

Looking around at the money exchanging hands, most of which would go into Hartman's pockets, Greeley observed, 'I find it difficult to place you, Mr Hartman. Your kind of business is surely better suited to the outlook of a man like Coles rather than people like James and Denis Moore. When the cattle trade dries up, as it surely will, you can pull down and move on to the next lively town.'

'I'm not a young man, Liam,' Hartman replied with a smile and a shake of his head. 'I see the Golden Wheel as my final venture in this kind of business. When the herds no longer come up the trail to Oaksworth I will become a senior citizen of the town, running something like a general store, even a gentleman's outfitters. For some years the West has been settling down, Liam, and I feel it high time that I did the same.'

Suspecting that Hartman was trying to influence him in some way with this conversation, possibly with the future in mind, Greeley said. 'I can't see myself as living here when the town has settled down, Mr Hartman. Oaksworth will then have nothing to offer a man who can do nothing but use his fists and a gun.'

'You put yourself down, Liam,' the saloon owner refilled both glasses. 'You are not a mindless bully-boy, a two-bit thug, or a gunman driven on by a killing lust. You have a good brain, son. The new Oaksworth will need you.'

Emptying his glass, Greeley put it on to the table with a clunk that had a finality about it. 'My brain isn't working too well right now. I have a town to patrol, which doesn't give me either the time or opportunity to work out the message you seem to be trying to give me. Pin it down, and I'll listen. Otherwise I'll be on my way right now.'

'Forgive me for being obscure,' Hartman said. 'My

fear is that putting it too bluntly might well push the
issue in the wrong direction. Very soon, Liam, you will
be called upon by circumstance to make a choice. All
that I ask, for myself and for Bill Bradford, who looked
upon you most fondly, is that you respond wisely.'

Standing up from where he had been sitting at the
table, Greeley replied seriously, 'If that time should
come, Mr Hartman, then I will come to you for advice.'

'I can assure you that the time *will* come, Liam, and
when it does there will not be time for discussion.'

Accepting this, promising that he would give it much
thought, Greeley raised a hand in a kind of farewell
salute to Hartman, then walked out, very conscious of
the white-haired man's gaze following him.

Turning left on his way to the American Playground,
Greeley paused as a woman's voice hissed cautiously at
him from the shadows.

'Marshal!'

Greeley waited for a moment to check out the
situation. He concentrated on the dark areas across the
street from where the woman had called. She could be
a decoy. If he walked towards her he might well get a
bullet in the back.

Satisfied that there were no threatening factors in the
situation, he walked to where the voice had come. In
the half light he could see a young and pretty woman
about whom there was a familiarity that put him at a
loss.

'You know who I am?' she asked pensively.

About to admit that he didn't, Greeley found her
identity clicked suddenly into his mind, and he tested it.
'You are the printer's wife?'

'Yes, I'm Peggy Evans,' she said, looking fearfully
around her as if the shadows held some menace.
'Please don't tell Clem, my husband, that I have spoken
to you.'

'A conversation between your husband and myself

isn't likely.' Greeley gave a little grin that was lost in the darkness. 'What can I do for you, ma'am?'

'We have two young children, a girl and a boy,' she told him instead of answering his question.

'So?' he shrugged.

Peggy Evans started to cry softly. 'My husband is very angry because that man Kennedy was freed instead of being punished. Clem blames you, Marshal, and he has sworn to get you. I'm asking you to save his life for me and our children, Marshal.'

'I have no argument with your husband, Mrs Evans, but if he tries to bushwhack me I will have to defend myself.'

Peggy Evans shook her head vigorously, her words chilling Greeley. 'He doesn't intend to shoot you in the back, Marshal. Clem is not like that. He is going to confront you on the street tomorrow, Marshal, face to face.'

This was grim news for Greeley. He had neither the desire nor any reason to kill Clem Evans. The printer was brave but misguided, seeing Greeley as the main problem in Oaksworth. If when Evans faced him Greeley should walk away, then that would shame the printer in front of the whole town. Yet to accept the challenge would mean killing a man who didn't deserve to die.

'What do you want me to do?' he asked the distraught woman.

'I don't know,' she confessed with a sob.

'You've sure got me beat with this, ma'am,' Greeley said, leaving her.

'Please do something, Marshal, I beg of you,' she cried after him.

It was asking too much of him, Greeley complained to himself as he entered the crowded American Playground. While prepared to face any tough who wanted to smash his face, and accommodate a fast gun seeking him out to gain notoriety, Greeley could not enter into a one-sided gunfight with a family man. It weighed heavily on his mind while he talked to Richmond Coles, but there was no point in discussing it with the saloon owner. Coles's solution would be to blast the angry printer into oblivion.

While taking a final drink for the night with Pat Brogan, before he retired to his bed at the jail, Greeley told her his problem.

'Marshal or not, Liam,' she said in alarm, 'if you gun down a man like that you'll be finished in Oaksworth.'

'I'll be finished completely,' he told her numbly. 'I can't kill Evans and live with myself afterwards.'

Holding up a hand for silence, Pat Brogan spent a few moments in deep thought, then came up with what could be the answer. 'It's tomorrow morning that he's coming for you, Liam?'

'According to his wife.'

With a nod, Pat said, 'Right. Now, you do something different every day, depending what has to be done. What is the only thing that you do each morning without fail?'

'Have breakfast here with you,' Greeley replied.

'Exactly, so it's my bet that Evans will call you out from here. It's so simple, Liam. I'll go out the front and tell him that you're not here, while you slip out the back, come up behind him and disarm him.'

Greeley liked the idea. Liked it a lot. Holding Pat to him, he said, 'You're real clever. That way Evans won't lose face. It will be me who will appear to be a coward sneaking up behind him.'

'Which won't worry you in the slightest,' she smiled fondly, giving him a hug.

The next morning everything began to happen in the way Pat Brogan had forecast that it would. Greeley was close to finishing his breakfast when Clem Evans shouted out in the street.

'You in there, Marshal? Come on out, Greeley!'

With Pat heading for the front door of the saloon, Greeley slipped out the back and went a full block along the rear of the buildings. He moved fast, wanting to get on to the street a fair distance behind Evans so as to evaluate the situation, work out exactly what had to be done, while Pat Brogan kept the printer in conversation.

On reaching the street and looking in the direction of Pat Brogan's saloon, Greeley was momentarily staggered by the scene in front of him. Pat had her back against the wall of her place, both hands clapped over her mouth in horror. Clem Evans had his back to Greeley, watching Rafe Kennedy advance towards him, arms held crooked, hands over his two guns in readiness.

Watching the people on the street scatter for cover, Greeley heard Evans's voice, made squeaky by distance. 'It's your boss I'm looking for, Kennedy, but I'll be happy to take you out first.'

Stepping out into the street, Greeley was powerless. Any attempt to intervene would have Evans turn his way, giving Kennedy an advantage that, as an experienced gunman, he had no need of. So he stood watching, feeling as if he'd been hog-tied and was rooted to the spot.

Kennedy's mirthless little chuckle reached Greeley. He saw the man with two guns, his body tense, advance relentlessly on the hapless Evans. Kennedy stopped, waiting. It was too far for Greeley to see, but he could imagine the wolfish grin the unpleasant face of Kennedy would be wearing.

Probably realizing in the last second that he had made a terrible mistake, Clem Evans went for his gun. His movement was abysmally slow, terribly clumsy. Evans's fingers had just made contact with the handle of the gun he wore in a holster attached to a too-high gunbelt, when Kennedy drew both guns and fired a shot from each.

Clem Evans spun like a top, the gyrations seeming to go on and on as a woman's piercing scream rent the air and Peggy Evans was running to her husband. Greeley ran, too. He saw Evans fall dead in the dust just before his wife reached him. Greeley watched her fall on top of her dead husband, crying and screeching. On his way he passed two bemused looking children. Holding hands, they were a boy and a girl, just as the worried woman had told him the previous night.

As Greeley reached the fallen Evans and his grieving wife, there were cries of, 'Arrest him, Marshal.'

Defying those who were demanding his arrest, and Greeley, Kennedy just stood there, his guns re-holstered, no smile on his face but just looking confident.

'I can't arrest him. It was self-defence,' Greeley told a scornful and irate crowd. Technically, in law, it was true. It was a moral crime only, for there had been no way that Evans could have beaten Kennedy to the draw.

'That is true,' Hugh Hartman supported Greeley from the outer edge of the crowd. 'Clem Evans drew first.'

'Even so, Kennedy,' Greeley told his deputy, 'I guess the best thing you can do is ride out of town, and stay away.'

'I've no reason to run,' Kennedy replied, and strolled off in the direction of the Golden Wheel.

Three women had gently lifted Peggy Evans from the body of her husband, and Ike Stevenson was coming forwards, measuring tape in his hand. Bob Marlin was heading for Greeley, who looked past the crippled boy to where his sister and Martha Jane stood surveying the grim scene, sadness on both of their faces. If they saw Greeley then neither of them showed any sign that they had done so.

'My plan didn't work, Liam,' Pat Brogan said softly and sadly from beside him.

'Nobody could have foreseen this happening,' he told her.

'That poor woman,' Pat said with a shiver, as Peggy Evans sobbed uncontrollably in comforting arms. 'That Kennedy's a bad one, Liam.'

Greeley didn't need telling this. Looking with hatred at the back of the departing Kennedy, he walked over to where the two Evans children unnoticed by the women who were caring for their mother, were kneeling beside their dead father, poking at the body curiously as Stevenson ignored them and carried on with his measuring. Bending, Greeley scooped them up, one in each arm, taking them back to where Pat Brogan stood.

Taking one of the children from him, the girl, she said, 'Let's take them over to my place until things are sorted.'

They were heading that way when two women saw them and came dashing their way. Faces red with anger and disgust, one of the woman snatched the child from Pat Brogan's arms while the other did the same to Greeley. As triumphant as if they had rescued the children from some contagious and vile disease, they carried the children to join a group of women who were looking with loathing and disgust at Pat Brogan and Greeley, most of their dislike focused on Pat.

Greeley was upset for Pat when he saw her walk away from the incident with her head drooping, tears glistening in her eyes.

'Don't let them worry you, Pat,' he advised.

'I don't,' she lied in reply. 'It doesn't matter about me, but those people expect you to risk your life to protect them, Liam, but they wouldn't give you the time of day in return.'

'It's just you and me against the rest of the world, Pat,' he joked to lighten the gloom that had settled on them.

But he was in a serious mood that evening when he

began his nightly patrol at the American Playground instead of at the Cattleman's Cottage. Stepping out of character, Greeley, who was known to be aloof by those who worked in the town's saloons and gambling houses, leaned his elbows on the bar to speak with a girl named Rita, who wore her long golden hair in ringlets.

After some conversation, Greeley surreptitiously passed Rita money. He touched her on her arm as he left her, and Rita nodded to confirm something and gave him a reassuring smile.

'Has Pat Brogan locked the door on you, Liam?' Coles, who had been watching the exchange, leered when Greeley joined him.

'Is that what she did to you?' Greeley enquired, enjoying the flash of anger his jibe had promoted in the saloon owner.

Before they could have any further conversation, a big-built cowboy walked to stand between them, facing Greeley. 'I hear tell, Marshal, that you're the hard man around here.'

'Somebody's been telling you lies,' Greeley replied. The cowboy was just drunk enough to be reckless, and Greeley wanted no diversions that night.

Unused to handling money, the cowboy now stood, his tongue protruding as he peeled banknotes from a roll. Placing the roll back into a shirt pocket, he put a little stack of creased notes on a table. Then he spoke loud enough to draw the attention that he wanted.

'There's twenty dollars that says I can whup your butt,' the cowboy said, grinning round at his gathering crowd of hopeful spectators.

'Some other time, cowpoke,' Greeley said, beginning to walk past the cowboy to get to the door.

'Hey . . .' the cowboy said, angry at being denied his chance to show how good he was.

As he said his one-word protest, the cowboy took one step forwards. Still walking, not turning his head to look at the persistent man, Greeley shot a right fist out sideways. It connected solidly with the cowboy's chin, sending him backwards, his bulk smashing tables and chairs, breaking glasses as it went.

As the heavy body of the unconscious man thudded to the floor, Greeley turned, walked back three paces, picked up the twenty dollars off the table, folding them before putting them in his pocket and going on out of the saloon.

Greeley did the remainder of his early round, but when he returned to Richmond Coles's saloon he went round the back instead of going inside. Leaning his back against a wall, hidden by the night, he waited patiently.

Ten minutes later he heard Rita's voice giggling loudly as she left the saloon. Greeley pushed himself away from the wall to stand upright, waiting. The bright colours of the girl's clothes showed up first, then Greeley gave an inaudible sigh of satisfaction as he saw she was accompanied by a man. He stepped out in front of them, separated by a few yards.

'Go, Rita,' he ordered, 'as quickly as you can.'

There was a curse from the man as the girl did as she was told, running awkwardly on feet more accustomed to the dance-floor than rough ground. When she was out of sight, Greeley stepped from the shadows, and the man left standing there breathed his name in disbelief.

'What's this, Greeley?' he asked.

'Exactly what it seems, Kennedy. Don't worry, I'll give you a chance to draw first, just like you did the printer.'

Kennedy spat his words out. 'I don't need no favours from you, Greeley.'

'You'll be doing me a favour,' Greeley said quietly. 'That's the way I want it, with you slapping leather first.'

Kennedy, who had been standing stiffly, arms spread,

suddenly gave a laugh and relaxed. 'This is loco, Greeley. What are we doing? We're both fast, Greeley, pretty damned fast. Could be we'll kill each other.'

'More likely that one will survive, Kennedy.'

'Why should even one of us die, Greeley, answer me that?'

'That's an easy one,' Greeley replied with what sounded like a chuckle. 'Because I want to kill you.'

'Could be that I'll kill you,' Kennedy pointed out.

'I don't see it that way.'

'You're good, Greeley, but not the best I've seen.'

'Maybe so, but I'm better than you,' Greeley said.

'I guess there's no way that I can make you change your mind?'

'There's no way, Kennedy.'

A dog barked somewhere in the town. Out in the flatlands a coyote seemed to do its best to reply. Taking advantage of the diversion, Kennedy went for his guns. He was fast, but Greeley shaded him. But as he saw his slug slam into Kennedy's chest, knocking him backwards, Greeley felt a burning sensation just below his left armpit. By the time he had made it back to Pat Brogan's saloon, his shirt was soaked with blood down the left side to the waist.

As soon as she saw him, Pat motioned him into a chair before going out of the room into the kitchen. When she came back, carrying a bowl of warm water and a flannel, Greeley had stripped himself to the waist and was wiping blood from his side with a neckerchief. Being wounded was a new experience for him.

'Don't get germs in the wound,' she ordered, moving his hand away and lifting his arm to survey the damage. 'You're lucky, Liam. The bullet passed under your arm, just grazing your ribs as it went by.'

Bathing the wound and washing the blood from the rest of his muscular torso, she asked softly. 'Rafe Kennedy?'

'Yes.'

The following morning when Kennedy's body was discovered, many people guessed, Rita the dance-hall girl was fairly certain, but only Pat Brogan and Liam Greeley knew for sure who had killed him.

NINE

Financial panic struck Kansas without warning, devastating Oaksworth. Drivers and shippers went immediately bankrupt when the cattle market collapsed suddenly. The few cowboys who found their way into town were owed wages by their employers and had nothing to spend. The saloons, gaming houses, hotels and boarding houses were starved of trade. Oaksworth changed, virtually overnight, from a bawdy, rowdy thriving cowtown into a kind of graveyard for the living. From Bob Marlin Greeley learned that his sister's restaurant was empty of diners, and Elizabeth Marlin feared that she would be forced to close down. Some of the tradesmen took a more optimistic view, saying that they believed the crisis would end, beef prices would pick up, and Oaksworth would once again come lustily to life. Hugh Hartman, Greeley learned, had a cautiously bright view of the future.

'I don't think the town will ever return to being the Oaksworth we have known, Liam,' the saloon owner replied when a worried Greeley asked. 'But this crisis could well hasten the establishment of the town as I, and others like me, want to see it.'

When Greeley made his way to the oddly quiet, barely patronized American Playground expecting to see Richmond Coles sitting gloomily amid his crumbling dreams. Greeley found that the reverse was the case. In conference with a group of strangers, opulent businessmen in frock coats and tall hats, Coles broke away to come up smilingly to Greeley, pumping him excitedly by the hand.

'We must feel free to congratulate each other, Liam. If we had been able to plan a crisis like this, then we couldn't have got it so absolutely perfect as this. It's ideal, Liam, absolutely ideal.'

Unable to grasp the reason for Coles's elation, because everyone else he had spoken to were both disappointed and disheartened by the financial collapse, Greeley kept his ignorance from Coles. He just nodded and waited for the saloon owner to expand on the subject. He didn't have long to wait.

'They're practically giving beef away down at the yards,' Coles said, then lowered his voice so that the businessmen, who were deep in conversation, couldn't hear. 'We have bought up just about every available head. This has speeded things up, Liam. Between you and me, these men are about to pour millions of dollars into setting up our own refrigerator car company. We buy cattle for just cents here, and ship them back East, frozen, where a fortune will be paid for them.'

Understanding now, disturbed to think that Coles and his financial investment associates were going to profit hugely from the distress of the broken men he had seen morbidly walking around the town, Greeley left. Coles's parting remark was that now he had secured all the cattle trade, owning all of the town was now his target.

'When people get over this fright, Liam, and money starts flowing once more,' Coles enthused, 'Oaksworth will become a goldmine. You'll be mayor of a mighty fine town then, Liam, and I won't be satisfied until every business on Main Street has my name above the door.'

Accustomed to Richmond Coles's bragging, Greeley let this slide past him, but he realized his mistake when the town came back to life, though in a very different way from before. He first knew about it when he rode back into town after a spell of gun practice down by the river. Surprised to see horses tied to the hitching rails of all the saloons and gambling dens, a puzzled Greeley had just dismounted when a breathless Bob Marlin ran up to him.

'Mr James Moore sent me to fetch you, Liam. There's big trouble over at the Cattleman's Cottage.'

Going to the Moore place with the crippled boy, Greeley grasped his shoulder and moved him to one side by the door. There was music and raucous laughter coming from inside, and then gunfire joined in with the din.

'Stay here, boy.'

It was packed when Greeley stepped inside. He took in everything within seconds. His posters had been torn from the walls. All of the men present, hard men, outlaws rather than cowboys, were armed. One of them, although staggeringly drunk, was displaying amazing accuracy with a six-shooter by shattering the bottles on the shelves behind the bar. Within seconds of Greeley's arrival, a bullet struck a huge mirror behind the bar, shattering it as the men in the bar cheered.

Skirting the crowd, the Moore brothers reached him, with James running a nervous tongue over his lips before he could manage to speak. 'This outrage has to be stopped, Marshal.'

Greeley shook his head, dismissing the idea of intervention. It was clear to him now that all of these men, and probably those in other saloons along Main Street, were in the employ of Richmond Coles and his backers. These rowdies had been brought in to drive the businessmen of Oaksworth out, leaving the town wide open for the Coles's faction.

'I can do nothing,' he shouted to Moore above a new uproar. It was true a man alone didn't have a chance here.

'That's not good enough, Marshal,' James Moore said, a mingling of fear and anger causing his eyes to twitch.

'Not good enough at all,' Denis Moore added.

'At least stop that man shooting at our property,' James Moore pleaded.

'If I try to,' Greeley told him, 'it will spark off a riot. Then you will lose everything, including your lives.'

Able to see the stark logic in this, James Moore said, 'We need outside help. I'm sending off a man right now to fetch the County Sheriff, Sam Kingsley.'

Barely hearing what Moore was saying, aware that no sheriff could do anything here, Greeley was regretting having thrown in his lot with Richmond Coles. Greeley hadn't envisaged anything like this happening. The town was out of control. It had passed into the hands of wild men brought in by Coles. Frustrated because he could do nothing on his own, Greeley left the Cattleman's Cottage and made his way to Pat Brogan's place.

Hearing the noise going on inside long before he reached a hitching rail crowded with horses, Greeley prepared himself to take on all comers if necessary to defend Pat.

But it didn't come to that. Although Pat's customers were the same rough type as those plaguing the Moore brothers, they seemed to have some kind of respect for Pat. Although unruly, they were drinking and gambling without transgressing the unspoken rules of the house. Remembering Pat Brogan's talk of a one-time relationship with Richmond Coles, Greeley guessed that Coles had given instructions that no one went too far in her place.

Coming up to him, her lovely face marred by worry,

she exclaimed. 'Liam! You're not going to try to control the town tonight, are you?'

'No,' he replied. 'As long as you are safe.'

'I'm safe,' she assured him. 'When they came bursting in here I feared it would be worse. What's it like in the other places?'

'I've only been to the Moores', and they're taking that place apart.'

'This is Richmond Coles's doing, you know that, don't you?' Pat enquired.

'I know, and I'll find a way round it,' Greeley said.

'Please be careful, Liam,' she begged.

'I will. I'll be back to see you later,' he said, pushing through a jostling mob to make his way to the door.

As he walked to the Grand Slam Greeley knew what had to be done. Coles had said that he had taken a chance for the first time in his life by forming a loose partnership with Greeley. It had been a mistake on Coles's part. He soon must learn that he shouldn't have taken the chance. The only way to save the town was for Greeley to kill Coles.

He found Jud Parkins faring much worse than Pat, and probably as badly as the Moore brothers. The harassed, sweating owner of the saloon was so busy trying to keep his bar staff and himself alive that he didn't see Greeley come in, take a quick look around, and then leave.

At the Golden Wheel it was absolute chaos. Hugh Hartman had ordered his bartenders out of the place, and had retired to his office, leaving his drunken, brawling customers to help themselves to drink. Peering out of the door, holding it just ajar, he spotted Greeley and beckoned for him to come and join him in the office. Greeley got through the mob successfully, and Hartman closed and bolted the door once he was inside the office.

'I expected something to happen, but not this,'

Hartman said, pouring himself and Greeley a drink as they both sat.

'I think that you've taken the right action,' Greeley observed.

'I'm sure that I have,' Hartman nodded a sorrowful head. 'I can put the place back together tomorrow by staying alive. Had I tried to protect it tonight I would be dead by now. What of you, Liam? You're not going to go up against this lot?'

'No, just the man who caused it all,' Greeley said. 'He took a chance on me, Mr Hartman, and I'm about to prove he was unwise.'

'Richmond Coles doesn't take chances,' Hartman trotted out what had become a hackneyed phrase.

'Not this time. Coles is no match for me.'

'No, that s true,' Hartman said softly, 'but Whitey Stein is, and he's Coles's man.'

Stumped for a moment, the truth then dawned on him, but to be certain he asked Hartman. 'The name you mentioned, did he get it because he has white hair, which he wears long?'

'That's Stein,' Hartman confirmed through taut lips. 'He's a cold-blooded killer, Liam. It's said that he's the fastest ever with a gun.'

It was coming together for Greeley now. Coles, professing to have a mutual agreement based on trust with Greeley, had his gunman in the background all the time.

'Fast or not,' he said, getting to his feet. 'I'm going to call on Coles right now.'

'You won t find him tonight, Liam. Coles has shut up shop until this little game of his is over.'

'He'll wait,' Greeley said as he let himself out of the office.

'Take care, Liam, take care,' Hartman called after him.

Outside he walked a short distance to take a look at

the American Playground, just to be sure. It was closed and in darkness, so Greeley turned and retraced his steps, passing Jud Parkins's place, noticing that, if anything, it was noisier than when he had previously gone by. In contrast, all activity in Pat Brogan's saloon seemed to have ended. There wasn't a sound coming from the place.

Going in, Greeley found the customers standing as still as statues. All eyes were fixed on the far end of the bar where Pat Brogan stood on a chair outside of the counter, holding a .38 inexpertly in both hands. The gun was aimed at a slim youngster who stood at the head of a gang of five toughs who were no older than himself.

'Drop her, Al,' one of the gang urged the leader.

But Al just stood there, posing with one shoulder a little higher than the other, an insolent smile on his not unhandsome face.

'Put the money back where it belongs,' Pat said through clenched teeth.

Greeley got the situation then. The bunch of five had snatched the night's takings, and Pat Brogan, as tough as ever, was determined to get it back. But she was in great danger. Greeley wanted to call to her but couldn't risk the consequences of doing so. But then he knew that he had to do something, but was totally helpless as he saw that she was squeezing on the trigger.

A shot sounded, loud and harsh in the confinement of the saloon. It wasn't Pat who had fired. From where he stood Greeley hadn't seen the boy named Al draw, but he was standing with a smoking gun in his hand as Pat, her right shoulder awkwardly twisted, shattered and bloody, dropped her .38 and seemed to be in danger of falling backwards off the chair and over the bar.

Somebody in the crowd shouted 'No!' but then there were two more shots from the little group behind the leader. A horrified Greeley saw the heavy slugs smash

Pat's slim body back off the chair. Going through the air, she tipped head over heels until her body hit a shelf of glasses behind the bar, shattering them before falling out of sight down behind the counter.

Pushing through the crowd, flattening two men with his fists to get through, Greeley leapt up on to the bar. He sprinted along it, taking everyone by surprise. Then one man recovered his wits to stretch out a hand in an attempt at tripping the marshal. Lifting his foot as he ran, Greeley brought it down on the man's wrist, hearing the shriek of pain as the bones of the arm cracked and splintered.

Then he was at the end, enraged further by the sight of Pat Brogan's blood on the wall and bar top. Al was standing there, still grinning, inanely so Greeley reached down with both hands to grip him by the head. Lifting the boy up off the floor, he swung him by the head, tossing him up into the air, catching him by the ankles as he came down. With a mighty swing, Greeley kept hold of the ankles and smashed the youth's head against the hard wood of the bar top. The skull split open like a melon before Greeley dropped the body by letting go of the ankles, then kicked the dead youth out so that he landed among his frightened and sickened friends.

A glance out of the corner of his eye told Greeley that Pat Brogan was beyond earthly help. Still standing on the bar he drew his gun to cover the four remaining members of the gang. They were looking up at him fearfully as they wiped with their hands frantically, trying to rid themselves of what had splattered on them from the broken head of their friend. It was an exercise that proved too much for one youngster, who was retching violently.

'You four, make your way to the door. Remember, I've got you covered all the way,' Greeley said, keeping to the top of the bar, pacing along it slowly. He told the hushed crowd. 'Any of you try to mix in, and I'll down you.'

The four youngsters made their way through the crowd, with Greeley warning them to stay close to the bar. A tall man, further back in the crowd, moved. He might have been going for a gun, he might not. Greeley didn't know and he didn't care. He fired once, punching a dark hole between the man's eyebrows. It was a good move that kept the remainder in the saloon cowed as he reached the end of the bar, with his four captives now by the door.

There was danger for him now, for the men in the bar had got over their initial shock and recognized that he was only one against many. Greeley was pondering on his next move, how to make it from the bar to the floor while also getting his four prisoners out of the door, when fate took a hand.

Someone from the far corner took a shot at him. The bullet came close, but missed. What the single shot did do was cause a panic. Nobody seemed certain as to who was shooting at whom. So Greeley added to the confusion by firing two shots over the heads of the crowd before leaping to the floor. With blows delivered to their heads with the barrel of his gun, and threatening thrusts of the muzzle of his .45, he got the four youths out into the night.

'Run,' he yelled at them but they refused, knowing that their comrades would spill out of the saloon to rescue them.

Greeley shot one in the leg, just below the knee. As he fell, Greeley told the others to help him up and run with him. Terrified now, they did as they were told.

Reaching the jail, Greeley had time to unlock the door and push his captives in before he heard many feet pounding up the road. Inside, he bolted and barred the door before taking his four prisoners and locking them in a cage. Going to the shuttered window, Greeley put an eye to one of the slits purpose-built into the shutters to allow the jail to be defended in the event of an attack such as now seemed imminent. A fair-sized crowd was advancing, back-lit by three flaring torches carried by men bringing up the rear.

Fetching himself a rifle from the firearms cupboard, aware of the futility of attempting to take on so many armed men, Greeley was determined to go down fighting. He would take as many as possible with him when he went.

But the crowd had halted and there was a lot of dialogue going on. He was too far away to hear the words, but Greeley assumed that the crowd lacked enthusiasm for attacking the jail. Revenge was a poor excuse, for everyone present had to be aware that the death of Pat Brogan had been murder.

From behind him came the weak moan of the man he had shot in the leg, and one of the other captives called, 'He's losing blood fast, Marshal.'

'Good,' Greeley called back coldly.

Outside he could see the front rank of the crowd turning, folding into those behind them until the whole mass of bodies had been reversed similar to the style of a marching band. Greeley reasoned that the decision to attack had not been cancelled but postponed. When the mob had been stirred up and pointed back in the direction of the jail, then they would come with guns blazing. But Greeley was confident that it wouldn't happened that night,

Putting the rifle back in the cupboard, he didn't lie on his cot because he knew sleep wouldn't come. He sat in a chair, hearing the injured man's groans grow weaker, ignoring the pleas for a doctor to be called that the other prisoners constantly made. Greeley was totally uncaring.

An hour before dawn he placed his few possessions on a laid-out bandanna, folded the corners over, then tied the ends to make a small parcel. He would be leaving Oaksworth penniless, as he had arrived. The money he had won fighting Cherokee Dave had been spent, and he had yet to receive one cent of his town marshal pay from the council. The high hopes he'd once held had been swamped by despair. All of it, everything he had done since coming to the town, had been pointless and fruitless. He would like to have questioned Uncle Elvir on what had gone wrong; possibly even blame him for it, but he hadn't for some time been aware of the old man being around. In the short time that Uncle Elvir had been dead even his memory had faded, to leave Liam Greeley feeling very alone.

When he stepped out into the deserted street a few silvery streaks to the east advertised the coming of a new day. A day when the mayor of Oaksworth would leave as he had arrived, riding the rods with the rest of the hoboes. But first Greeley had his respects to pay. No, it was more than that, but he wasn't learned enough in such things to identify what it really was.

The sky was lightening enough when he reached Ike Stevenson's place for Greeley to find his way to the rear of the premises. The heavy back door was unlocked. It creaked complainingly on unoiled hinges, and he left it wide open when he walked inside. Pausing for his eyes to accustom themselves to the dim light, he saw a pine box and walked to it. There was no lid, and he found himself looking down at the smashed head of the man he had killed when in a cold rage, the youth named Al.

Greeley found Pat Brogan lying in a box roughly in the centre of the rickety lean-to. Looking at her, he wondered if he had made yet another mistake by coming here. In no way could he equate the still figure with its eyes closed though in a very different state from sleep, with the energetic, laughing, serious, tough but generous Pat Brogan that he had been so close to.

A yellow light dancing outside and intruding into the shed caught his eye. Hand instinctively going towards his gun, he pulled it back and hooked the thumb in his belt. Liam Greeley had even lost the natural desire for self-preservation.

Ike Stevenson came in cautiously through the door, holding a storm lantern aloft with his left hand, carrying a cumbersome scatter-gun in his right. He was so relieved to see Greeley that he made a couple of choking noises before he was able to speak.

'Oh, it's you, Marshal.'

As the carpenter approached the glow from his lamp brought an animation to the girl in the pine box for Greeley, but it was only a momentary illusion. The body swiftly went back to being a not very apt symbol of the Pat Brogan he had known and loved.

'Just as purty a picture now as she ever was, Marshal,' Stevenson commented, whispering as if it was possible to awaken some of his temporary boarders. 'I fixed her up best I could, just as she deserved.'

Stevenson went out then, leaving Greeley alone once more. He found himself searching for something that wasn't there. Greeley would have probably spent all day waiting to find whatever it was, if the pounding of hooves and wild shouting hadn't reached him from out on Main Street.

Hurrying out, he went to the front of the building. Others had come from their homes, too. He saw the two Moore brothers, Hugh Hartman, several other businessmen and, standing side by side, standing in close to the front wall of the Cattleman's Cottage, Bob and Elizabeth Marlin together with Martha Jane. They had all come out to be spectators with Greeley as riders, those from last night or others very similar, swung off Main Street and headed for the jail.

All carrying rifles, they dismounted in a cloud of dust and rushed the building. Kicking in the door, they entered and brought out the four prisoners, carrying one. From the distance Greeley couldn't tell if the fourth man was dead or alive.

Mounting up, they lassoed various projections on the building, whooping, shouting as they rode a little way off, pulling sections of the jailhouse down as they did so. When nothing else could be pulled down, they fired the place. Riding round and round, their horses rearing and shrieking, the riders enjoyed the blaze. Then as thick black smoke billowed up, they tired of their game and rode back down to Main Street.

The residents vanished, and Greeley, alone on the street, pulled back out of sight as the large gang divided themselves up between the town's saloons. Hitching their horses, they kicked in the doors of the Cattleman's Cottage, the Grand Slam and the Golden Wheel. Greeley was glad that they didn't go near to Pat Brogan's place. Had they done so, then he would have intervened. As a result, facing so many guns, he would never leave Oaksworth.

Now that the menacing riders had cleared the street, the citizens of Oaksworth were cautiously venturing out again, looking aghast at the burning jail. Catching sight of Greeley, James Moore walked to him, his brother close behind.

'What is going to happen to Oaksworth, Marshal?' James Moore asked.

'It's disastrous,' Denis Moore whined.

Hugh Hartman walked up as Greeley replied, 'The choice is yours, Moore. You can either fight for the place or let it go.'

'We are traders, merchants, not gunfighters, Greeley,' James Moore protested angrily. 'We pay you to do the fighting.'

'You've overlooked two things, Moore . . .' Greeley began, but Hartman filled in for him.

'We haven't paid Liam a cent, James,' the elderly

saloon owner said.

'That can be rectified,' Moore said firmly. 'I'll see that you get everything owing to you, within the hour. Now, what was the second item you mentioned, Greeley?'

'I can't do it alone. You people of Oaksworth will have to arm yourselves and give me backing.'

'Out of the question . . .' James Moore was saying, but Greeley had spotted some furtive movements at the rear of Ike Stevenson's premises.

Slipping away before Moore could notice that he had gone, Greeley went round the back of the building. When he saw Richmond Coles tugging at the back door of Stevenson's, Greeley hissed a warning. 'Don't go in there.'

Alarmed, shaking a little with fear at the sight of Greeley, Coles used both hands to open his coat wide. 'I'm unarmed, Liam. I didn't plan this. Pat was the last person I would wish to see hurt.'

'Nevertheless, she wouldn't want you in there,' Greeley said.

'Since when have you been able to speak for the dead,' Coles challenged, courage slowly returning because Greeley hadn't gone for his gun.

'Since I started mixing with them, Coles. Whatever you say, and though I know that you didn't fire the bullets, you killed Pat Brogan.'

'There's no way that I can convince you otherwise, Liam,' Coles said, regretfully. 'So, if you're going to kill me, get it over with.'

Accepting that this was bravado on the part of Coles, who knew that Greeley wouldn't shoot him down while unarmed, a Greeley who suddenly became very tired of it all, told him, 'Stay away from here, Coles. Go back to your own place. If you should ever see me again, then make sure that you're carrying a gun, for I'll kill you regardless.'

Coles walked off and Greeley went into the shed, took a final look at Pat Brogan, then picked up the bundle of possessions he had left there and went back out on to the street.

More of the townsfolk were on the street now, and additional riders had come in. Some joined the earlier arrivals in the saloons, while others just loitered as if expecting something to happen that would involve them.

The two Moores, Hugh Hartman, Jud Parkins, and a few of the town's merchants had formed themselves into a kind of deputation, with James Moore once again being the spokesman.

'What are your plans now, Marshal?'

Resting his bundle on a post, Greeley was about to answer when a crashing of breaking glass followed by the tinkling of falling shards came from up the street. Three of the riders who were strangers to the town had kicked in the window of a store and were helping themselves to the goods inside.

'That's my place,' one of the merchants cried. A small, balding man, he was stopped from running back to his store by Hugh Hartman grabbing his arm.

'Take it easy, Philip, take it easy,' Hartman advised soothingly.

Concern showing on his face, James Moore looked away from the ongoing looting and back to Greeley. 'Well, Marshal, what do you intend to do.'

'I'm no longer marshal here,' Greeley said, picking up his bundle, gesturing with it towards the railway yards. 'The next train that leaves here, I'll be riding on it.'

He saw the fear, naked and agonizing on their faces as they contemplated being left without his gun. Greeley found it possible to feel sorry for them, but not sorry enough to be prepared to stand alone against the lawless element Richmond Coles had brought into the town. It was a situation with so many wrong turns that it had become an emotional maze. Coles must have thought a lot of Pat Brogan to have sneaked down to Stevenson's to say goodbye to her. No doubt he hadn't predicted, or wanted her death, and he must be bitterly regretting it now. Greeley accepted that he was personally far from being beyond reproach. Martha Jane Ackerman had come out here all the way from New York to be with him, and he was about to abandon her.

Hardening himself against any last-minute weaknesses, he had his bundle under his arm, turning away, when his name was called challengingly.

'Greeley!'

Coming back round, ready to meet any situation, not really caring what he had to face, Greeley had to blink twice in quick succession. With a gun held in his good arm, aimed directly at Greeley was Bob Marlin, anger blazing in his eyes. It was an ageing 'Chassepot' infantry rifle, but it was breech-loading and capable of dealing out instant death.

Behind Greeley came the sound of another building being broken into, but a determined Bob Marlin was not distracted as Greeley had hoped.

'You're not going anywhere, Greeley. We're not going to let you walk out on Martha Jane,' the crippled boy said evenly.

TEN

Greeley could hear more activity going on up Main
Street behind him. Other riders must have come into
town, but Bob Marlin didn't let his steady, angry gaze
stray from Greeley, and he still held the gun one-handed
but firmly. Behind the crippled boy Greeley could see
his sister standing beside Martha Jane, both of them
watching anxiously. Elizabeth Marlin's lips were
moving rapidly, and Greeley guessed she was either
saying a prayer or silently asking him not to harm her
brother. It was a situation such as he had never before
met. Although he could draw and finish Bob before the
boy could awkwardly pull the trigger, Greeley was
prepared to die from a bullet fired by the ancient rifle
rather than do that. With all his physical disadvantages,
Bob Marlin had the guts to face him. Having
previously liked the boy, Greeley was now filled with
admiration for him. Yet he saw no way out of this.

A sound of splintering timber and breaking glass
came from the rear of the Cattleman's Cottage.
Elizabeth ran to investigate, a hesitant Martha Jane
behind her. They came back, with Elizabeth screaming
out, 'They're smashing up my restaurant!'

Bob was affected by his sister's cry, and Greeley saw
the boy wavering. Dropping his bundle on to the
ground, Greeley said tersely. 'Take the rifle off me,

boy.'

Delaying for only a second, Bob Marlin lowered the rifle and hurried over to put his good arm comfortingly around his sister's shoulders as Greeley called out a question, 'How many are there, Elizabeth?'

'Five, maybe six,' the girl shouted back.

Greeley cursed under his breath. The sawn-off shotgun he needed had perished in the fire at the jail. He faced the merchants who were lined up beside the Moore brothers.

'Any of you men keep shotguns and buckshot in your store?'

'I do, Marshal,' a tall, bent-over man said. 'But it's up the street there to the left, just where those men are doing the shooting.'

The men he referred to were a group of rowdies who were laughing hysterically as they fired into the ground around the feet of one of their own number, causing him to dance wildly while at the same time complaining furiously.

'Have you the key?' Greeley asked, and when the merchant gave a nervous nod, he said, 'Come on.'

Putting himself as a shield between the merchant and the men firing guns, Greeley got them both almost to the shop when the men saw them and turned to enjoy some different fun, their guns still in their hands. Drawing fast, Greeley hit one who had not quite turned away from the man he had been making dance. As Greeley's bullet went home, a reflex action had the man squeeze the trigger of his gun, hitting the friend he had been firing at for amusement. Both men fell dead to the ground, alarming the rest so that they turned and ran.

Inside the store, Greeley waited impatiently while the owner unlocked a rack and passed him a shotgun. Breaking open a box of cartridges, Greeley filled his pockets to overflowing. Taking a spare box with him, he said, 'Come on, move,' and ran with the store owner back to where the other townsfolk stood apprehensively as the smashing and crashing went on in Elizabeth's restaurant.

Running the layout of the place through his mind, Greeley clutched the shotgun, having dropped the spare box of cartridges by his bundle, and ran along the side of the building. As he approached a window he launched himself into the air, rolling up into a ball as he crashed through, shattering the glass and the wooden sash.

Rolling as he hit the floor, he came up on to his feet among a bunch of men. They had been destroying tables and chairs, enjoying themselves as they did so. Now they became a tableaux of five statues, smiles frozen on their faces. There was a shattering roar as Greeley pulled the trigger of the shotgun. Buckshot ripped the smile off the face of a large red-haired man, taking most of his head with it at such close range. Panicked by what had happened to their buddy, the four rushed out of the door into an alley, with Greeley reloading the shotgun as he followed.

Moving smoothly now, glad of the action that was allowing him to fight back at last, Greeley knew that the four men were too far ahead for buckshot to be effective. So he drew his .45, to send one man pirouetting, slamming into a wall from which he slid lifeless to the ground as his three companions rounded the corner into temporary safety.

Shotgun held high, Greeley charged into Main Street, yelling at everyone, Elizabeth and Martha Jane in particular, 'Get off the street!'

He went up the street at a fast walk then. Up ahead he saw men who were looting a store lean out to ask the running three what the problem was. If they did get a warning answer, Greeley gave them no time to heed it. Jumping into the store, firmly placing his feet in the debris caused by the looting, he blasted one man in the middle with the shotgun, coming close to cutting him in two. As a second man ran, Greeley caught the shotgun by the barrel to deliver a crunching upward blow with the butt into the man's groin. Making only a deep grunt, the man doubled over and Greeley swung the shotgun up again to smash it into the man's face. As a third man went past him, Greeley drew and fired just as the man jumped high to get through the window. Greeley's bullet caught him in the leg, so that when he landed outside it was face down in the dust, where he lay writhing in agony.

Reloading the shotgun as he ran, Greeley fired at a man who had unhitched his horse from a rail. But the rider had wheeled the horse and brought it up on its rear legs to protect him. The buckshot peppered the neck and face of the horse. As it dropped down back on to all fours, Greeley drew his six-shooter and blew the man out of the saddle.

Stampeded by fear, driven on by the pain of its buckshot-lacerated head and neck, the horse charged wildly and noisily around Main Street, adding to the pandemonium.

Two men came out of the Golden Wheel, their steps made uncertain by drink. When Greeley blasted one of them against the wall of the saloon with buckshot, then drew again to kill the other man as he tried to run to his horse, it became a rout. With the crazed horse screaming as it dashed aimlessly around, there was enough fear generated for men to run out of just about every building to mount up recklessly and acrobatically in their eagerness to get out of town.

As they went, Greeley shot one more with his .45, seeing the rider slump over but not fall out of the saddle. Reloading the shotgun, he checked out every building, but there were none of the strangers left in Oaksworth. Coming out on to the street, the injured horse went by him in its crazy, zigzag flight. It did a figure of eight, giving Greeley the opportunity to judge when it would next be close to him. With his gun ready, he sent a single bullet into the animal's head as it went by. Amazingly it almost completed another figure of eight before the message that it was dead reached its brain, and it dropped like a stone.

Waiting until the dust cleared, Greeley looked up Main Street. Not far away, leaning relaxed against a post outside the neighbouring building to the American Playground, was a figure of a man distinctive by shoulder length white hair. Standing to look at the man for some half a minute, Greeley then turned, tucked the shotgun comfortably under his right arm, and walked back down to where the townsfolk had gathered outside the Cattleman's Cottage. Not looking at anyone other than Bob Marlin, Greeley passed the crippled boy the shotgun.

'It's loaded, Bob. You protect Elizabeth, Martha Jane and the others while I'm gone,' Greeley instructed, pointing to the box of cartridges on the ground by his bundle. 'There's more cartridges there if you should need them.'

The crippled boy nodded solemnly, thrilled by the trust shown in him by Greeley. He asked, 'Where are you going, Liam?'

Making no reply, Liam Greeley turned and walked slowly back up Main Street. Keeping to the centre of the street he passed the bodies of those he had killed. They lay at various angles, some of them twisted, having died in mid-movement. Greeley felt no stirring of regret. They had been men intent on destroying the lives of others, and he had simply reversed the situation they had created.

He could see Whitey Stein now, still leaning lazily against the same post. As Greeley closed the distance between them, Stein pushed himself upright to walk to the centre of the street facing Greeley. The moment of truth, Uncle Elvir, Greeley said wryly inside his head, your years of instruction and my abilities are about to be put to the test.

Stein said nothing. His face was expressionless as Greeley came closer. Hearing a slight sound of movement far behind him, Greeley assumed that it was the faithful Bob Marlin coming up to find a safe observation point.

Coming to a halt, staring into the white-haired man's peculiar, somehow opaque eyes, Hugh Hartman's voice echoed in his head, saying how fast this man was with a gun. Then Uncle Elvir was back, pushing Hartman out by reiterating the lessons of old. Obeying, Greeley had already aimed. All that remained was the draw.

Minutes went by with them facing each other. The tension was building high and fast. Affected by it, Greeley couldn't read any sign that said it was getting to Stein. A contest of life and death had become second to a matter of prestige. Neither of them was prepared to be the first to slap leather.

The delay was causing Greeley intolerable strain. He was aware that he would have to draw before another half second went by. But the white-haired man broke before he did. Stein went for his gun. He was so fast that it wasn't possible to separate his hand contacting the handle of his .45 from when it was held waist high, pointing at Greeley, a bullet leaving just ahead of the sharp crack and thin wisp of smoke.

Greeley just shaded Stein, and this saved his life. His bullet found Stein's heart a split second before the white-haired man had fired. The impact had knocked Stein's right hand slightly off aim, and his bullet went through the fleshy part, just below the ribs, of Greeley's left side, tearing a larger hole in his back as it exited.

Feeling no pain right then, although aware that he had been hit, Greeley watched as Stein's right wrist drooped crookedly and the gun slid from his fingers to fall into the dust, preceding his collapsing body by only a short space of time.

'Liam' the crippled boy called, and Greeley could hear his footfalls running towards him.

'Stay back, Bob!' he ordered.

The nerves around his wound, cut and numbed by the bullet, were coming back to life. A searing pain filled his left side from his shoulder down to below his hip as Greeley made his way towards the American Playground. Before entering he turned his head to ensure that the crippled boy wasn't near. Bob Marlin stood at the centre of the street, staring down at the dead Stein, and then up at Greeley.

Stepping inside the door of the saloon, Greeley paused to adjust to the half light caused by the shutters on the windows. In the light of two oil lamps placed at a distance from each other on the bar, he saw Richmond Coles, his elbows on the bar, leaning comfortably with a bottle and glass in front of him. It was obvious that he had been expecting Greeley.

'Liam, I'm glad that you came,' he called in a friendly way. 'I've been wanting to see you. Kansas is just about to emerge from its financial difficulties. The bad times are over, Liam, and we are on our way up. Come, join me in a drink and we'll plan our plans.'

Walking towards Coles, Greeley asked, 'Are you wearing a gun as I asked you to, Coles?'

'What is all this nonsense, Liam?' Coles asked in a tone that indicated he was both surprised and hurt. 'You are very wrong to believe that I would harm Pat in any way.'

'Are you wearing a gun, Coles?'

'For God's sake, Liam, what's the matter with you. The town is wide open, waiting for us to move in. There's a fortune to be made, and you can be the top man in Oaksworth.'

'I'm not interested,' Greeley said. 'Now, for the last

time, Coles, are you wearing a gun?'

Although not expecting Coles to have any back-up now that Stein was dead, Greeley took the precaution of checking out the surroundings. Satisfied that Coles and he were alone, he saw a stack of long torches propped in a corner, treated and ready to light. If evidence of Coles's involvement in the wrecking of the town was needed, which it wasn't, the torches would provide it. Hand above his holster, Greeley saw Coles step back slowly from the counter. Now conscious of warm blood seeping out of his wound, saturating his clothing around that area, Greeley's anger was boosted by a memory of another recent wound, an injury that Pat Brogan had so willingly and tenderly treated.

Opening his jacket, an uncertain smile on his face, Coles said. 'There you are, Liam, no gun.'

'Then get one, Coles, now!'

'You must think I'm mad, Greeley,' Coles exclaimed, dropping his smile and friendliness. 'If I was wearing a gun you'd have killed me by now.'

'What's the difference?' Greeley shrugged. 'I'm going to kill you anyway. I just wanted it to be fair, as we'd both be the same size behind guns.'

Moving forwards as he spoke, Greeley streaked out his left hand and caught Coles with a stinging backhand slap to the face that instantly drew blood from the mouth and nose. Staggered and angry, the lithe Coles sprang at Greeley to catch him a hard left and right punch to the face. There was no danger for Greeley in the blows, but they did have a momentary stunning effect. For a moment Greeley was at a loss. He had never fought a man lighter than himself, so Coles's agility was off-putting. But he got his fighting brain together as Coles showed courage in facing up to him.

Feinting with a left to Greeley's face, Coles then bobbed down, weaved to his right to throw a power-driven right hand into the bleeding wound in Greeley's side. Hurt, Greeley stepped back, lifting his arms to take a flurry of blows Coles had intended for his head. The realization that Coles had considerable experience in fisticuffs made it easier for Greeley, making him recognize that he had been holding back against a lighter man who was not a pugilist.

As Coles came in once more, aiming a looping right hand at Greeley's jaw, Greeley stepped inside, letting it go harmlessly round the back of his head as he drove a twisting left hook deep into Coles's stomach. Bringing that left hand up, fingers outstretched, Greeley flicked Coles under the chin, lifting his head up and back. The right fist that Greeley pounded into Coles's throat sent the lighter man backwards across the room until he slammed up against a wall, choking and gagging, going purple in the face.

Moving forward fast, taking short, sure steps, Greeley let his right hand go once more, aiming the fist for Coles's face. Even before Greeley released it he knew that it was a killer punch. His knuckles drove Coles's face in as the back of his head thudded dully against the wall. Turning away, hearing the man slump to the floor behind him, Greeley didn't need to look to know that he was dead.

Going to the bar, he swept along it with his arm to send the two lighted lamps crashing to the floor. They spilled oil and flames, igniting the floorboards, spreading flames across to lick at the furniture as Greeley walked to where the torches were stacked in a corner. One at a time he threw them into the growing fire, each one boosting its intensity. When he had used all of the torches and the American Playground was burning fiercely, Greeley walked out of the saloon.

Bob Marlin was waiting for him in the street. Concern showing on his thin face, the boy looked at his bloody wound but said nothing. He walked beside Greeley down Main Street to where the townsfolk waited. The burning saloon crackled. Occasionally there was a small explosion from inside. An acrid stench filled the air, reaching the far end of the street at about the same time as Greeley.

Elizabeth and Martha Jane wore expressions of alarm as they saw his blood-sodden shirt. Martha Jane started towards him involuntarily, but got hold of herself and stayed back. Not looking at any of them, Greeley bent, holding his injured side, to pick up his bundle of possessions. No one spoke to him, but as he was turning away conversation started to buzz and the crowd began discussing the fire and the killings.

From among the small group of town dignitaries, Hugh Hartman commented, 'It seems that we have to start Oaksworth all over again, just about from scratch. How are we to go about it.'

Greeley was walking away, heading for the railway yards, his bundle under his arm, when he heard James Moore answer Hartman. 'We should start by asking the town mayor.'

There was something in the way the businessman said this that made Greeley stop. Perhaps it was really Uncle Elvir who stopped him, and it was definitely the old man who made him turn to look back. James Moore was looking at him, shamefaced, trying to force a smile.

'Yes, Mr Greeley, I meant you,' he said.

'That's a fact,' Denis Moore said in support of his brother.

'We will understand if you refuse, Marshal,' James continued, 'but we would like you to stay.'

'The town would be honoured to have you,' Hugh Hartman said sincerely. 'And I would be honoured if you would allow me to shake the hand of a real man.'

Delaying for only a moment, Greeley shifted his bundle to his left arm, then stepped back to shake Hugh Hartman by the hand. It was a gesture that broke the ice, and everyone was coming forward to shake

Greeley's hand.

Elizabeth and Martha Jane were standing close by now, and the former said, 'You look as if you could use a good meal, Liam. When the doctor's seen to that wound I'll have dinner ready.'

Greeley nodded, happy to have been accepted back into the fold. Martha Jane was looking at him now, wanting to speak but too afraid to do so, while Greeley was desperate to speak to her, but didn't know what to say. As Bob Marlin fussed around, tugging with his good arm at Greeley, wanting to get him to the doctor, Martha Jane blurted out the words she had bottled up.

'I'll be waiting, Liam, if you want me.'

'I do,' he told her, ashamed at having treated her so badly, blaming the town and its people, but fully aware that the major fault had been his.

There was an ecstatic smile on her sweet face as she stood watching him walk off, weak from loss of blood now, leaning on the crippled boy a little as they went. But Greeley stopped and walked back to the girl unsupported. Wanting no more misunderstandings, nothing else to go wrong, he told her truthfully and sorrowfully, 'I have a burial to attend to first, Martha Jane.'

'I know. I'll be here when it's over, Liam.'

As Greeley walked away from her to rejoin Bob Marlin, a loud creaking, splintering noise filled the street as the roof of the American Playground fell in. Minutes later the whole building collapsed. There was some ragged clapping and a few cheers from the crowd. Liam Greeley didn't turn his head. He walked on in the knowledge that he would have to lay his ghosts before he could join the living to enjoy the exciting prospects offered by Oaksworth.